An Informal Introduction
by Heather Gray

I0551922

an Informal Romance novel

<u>Informal Romance Books</u>

An Informal Christmas

An Informal Arrangement

An Informal Introduction

An Informal Date (coming Fall 2016)

An Informal Affair (coming Spring 2017)

Unless otherwise noted, all Scripture quotations are taken from the HCSB®, Copyright © 1999, 2000, 2002, 2003, 2009 by Holman Bible Publishers. Used by permission. HCSB® is a federally registered trademark of Holman Bible Publishers.

Cover design by Heather Gray.
Cover art photos ©goodluz/Fotolia and ©VILevi/Fotolia. Used with permission.

Published in the United States of America by Heather Gray
www.heathergraywriting.com

Publisher's Note: This novel is a work of fiction. Names, characters, places, and incidents are either products of the author's imagination or used fictitiously. All characters are fictional, and any similarity to people living or dead is purely coincidental.

in celebration of my Savior
in memory of my daughter
with pride in my son
with gratitude for my husband

We know that in all things God works for good of those who love him, who have been called according to his purpose.

Romans 8:28

One

As if the flashing lights in her rearview mirror weren't enough, the trooper turned on the siren, too. Lily cringed and slid down in her seat like a teenager hiding from prying eyes. Of course, her teen years were long behind her, and any eyes intent on prying would need night vision goggles to see her. The sun hadn't yet kissed the eastern horizon.

She slowed and sought a place to pull over, no small feat on this narrow stretch of Lee Highway. Spotting a patch of grass to her right, she steered her silver two-door sedan as far over as she could and cut the engine. Her fingers drummed a rhythmless beat on the steering wheel as she waited for the trooper. He was probably busy checking with dispatch to make sure she wasn't a mass murderer. Because, clearly, rampaging homicidal maniacs drove nondescript cars on the way to the hospital in the wee hours of the morning.

In all her years traversing this road, Lily had never seen a state trooper on this particular stretch. Until today. Good thing she'd left early for work.

Thank you, God, for getting me up and out the door when You did.

The trooper climbed out of his cruiser and approached her parked vehicle. She hit the button and listened to the almost imperceptible hum as her window slid down. The grey of his uniform would have blended into the night were it not for the illumination of his headlights and his car-mounted spotlight. As it happened, they blinded her enough that she couldn't catch much more than the color of his clothes and a hint of his shape.

"License and registration, please." The voice was impatient. Tired, too. He was probably at the end of his shift, which meant she had little chance of winning the argument, but she wouldn't let that stop her from trying.

"I wasn't speeding."

"License and registration, please."

So much for the *serve* part of public service.

"Can you at least tell me why you pulled me over?"

"Give me your license and registration, ma'am."

Heat swept through Lily. It's not like she'd asked a difficult question. "How do I even know you're a state trooper and not some crazed rapist who's trying to get my address so he can break into my home?"

The trooper's shadowed mouth hinted at a smile, and his eyes morphed from intense pinpoints to... Hm. Eyes couldn't be huggable, could they?

Who was she kidding? She couldn't even see his eyes. Her imagination had to be on overdrive.

"Well, ma'am, most people consider those flashing red and blue lights as proof enough that I'm one of the good guys, but if it would make you feel better, I'd be happy to go turn the siren back on, too. I doubt crazed rapists announce themselves with police sirens." Now that he was speaking in actual sentences, Lily picked up a hint of honeyed Southern drawl dancing along the edge of his words. She never could resist Southern charm — real or imagined.

"Here." She handed him her driver's license and the other paperwork from her glove compartment.

He examined both and called her license information in, using the small radio strapped to his left shoulder.

"For the record, I did nothing wrong."

He stepped back from her car and listened carefully to whoever was on the other end of the radio. If it was even a real person. The garbled, static-like squawking left that in doubt.

Once the radio quieted, the trooper began entering information into a form held in place on his clipboard.

Fantastic. It was never good when they started writing. Not that she had enough experience to know…

The trooper finished what he was doing and approached her window. "I'm afraid you were driving recklessly, ma'am, swerving all over the road. You're going to step out of the car and do a field sobriety test for me."

"You're kidding, right?"

The light cast by his cruiser illuminated half his face. It was enough for her to catch the widening of his eyes at her response, but it did so with a blinding glare, preventing her from making out the details of his features. "No, ma'am, I'm not joking. Please exit the car and keep your hands where I can see them."

Lily opened her door and, keeping both hands in plain sight, climbed out. "How long have you lived around here?"

The trooper ignored her question. He indicated the barely-there white stripe on the edge of the road. "I need you to walk straight down this line from your car to mine." He remained between her and the cruiser but off to the side, presumably so he wouldn't block the onboard camera filming the entire incident.

Great. She only hoped she didn't become part of some viral video about drunken nurses. True or not, it could cost her the job she loved.

She walked the line with nary a wobble. The trooper made notations on his clipboard and gave her more commands. "Touch your nose with your left index finger."

She completed each of the tasks assigned her until, at last, he produced the electronic contraption from his car. "Take a deep breath and blow into this piece here."

He indicated the straw-like attachment he'd just put on. At least she got a clean one. That was something.

With a shudder, Lily shook the thought away and did as he'd instructed.

The trooper frowned at her. "You're not drunk."

"Of course not. I was swerving to avoid all the badly-patched potholes. This road is torture on every vehicle that's ever driven it, except for the snow plows which are responsible for most of the potholes to begin with." She was only getting started. "Then spring comes, and all the holes are fixed, but this year they must have used someone new because there's not a level patch anywhere in sight. There's not a suspension system out there that can compensate for this road."

"You know the potholes and bumps so well that you can swerve around them?"

He remained cast in shadow by their position, his back to the cruiser and its too-bright lights while she stood in front of him with the glare directly in her eyes. Lily was close enough now to make out some of the geography of his face — like his square jaw — but she still couldn't identify much beyond that. Certainly not enough to tell if she was being mocked or admired. "I drive the road on my way to work. It's faster than the freeway, which is always bogged down by now. And I never once swerved out of my lane. How is it any different than if I'd been trying to avoid debris? I wasn't being unsafe. I was swerving specifically so I *could* drive safely."

The trooper scratched his head, and Lily took a moment to admire his plentiful — if short — hair. The color remained indistinguishable, but at least he wasn't bald.

Not that bald was always bad. On some men, though, it was… unfortunate.

He shook his head and moved closer to show her the clipboard. "I'm giving you a warning. As far-fetched as it sounds, your excuse might just be legit. I need you to sign and date here."

Excuse? Lily tried not to growl as she grabbed the pen from him and completed her part of the form. "Any chance you'll hang back for a while?" Like, give her a ten-minute head start before making his way from the shoulder back onto the highway? Now that she was running late for work — thanks to him — she'd have to push the speed limit.

"In a hurry?"

She shrugged and withheld the glare she wanted to give him as she reached a hand out for her copy of the warning. "I wasn't before, but I am now."

"Wherever you're in a rush to go, I'm sure it's not life or death. Drive safe and follow the laws of the road. Including the speed limit."

Lily held back the mock salute she wanted to offer him. He'd gotten her morning off to a doozy of a start, but she'd do her best not to take it out on him. She could empathize, after all. Her job was to help people, too, and it sometimes required her to call people out on their behavior or habits. It wasn't fun to be cast in the role of *bad guy* in order to do good for people.

With a glance at the road, Lily buckled her belt. In the time they'd been on the shoulder, the highway had turned from a ghost town into a quagmire of early morning traffic. Making it to work on time was out of the question now. With a disgruntled mutter, she tucked the earpiece into place and hit a button on her steering wheel. "Call ICU." It was time to tell the charge nurse she would be late.

"Pulled over for drunk driving?"

Lily hung her head as she scrubbed in at the sink.

"Child, you have the kind of luck that gives most folks hound dog jowls." Lyza, the nurse she was scheduled to replace, leaned against the wall next to her and waited.

Could anyone talk to Lyza and not smile? "I don't own a hound dog, and hopefully I never develop jowls, but I appreciate the sentiment. I was supposed to get here early, too. Sorry they made you stay late for me."

With the lift of a shoulder, Lyza dismissed it. "No worries. I'm off the next three nights, and the extra thirty minutes was worth it to hear your story." The older nurse chuckled again. "Drunk driving. Unbelievable."

Lily would face a day full of good-natured ribbing about her escapades with a state trooper, but she didn't mind. Life in ICU could be wrapped up with a single word: intense. Being the occasional butt of a joke only meant people had something to laugh about. Tomorrow it would be somebody else's turn to lighten the mood with their own embarrassing story.

Lyza gave her the rundown. "Mr. Miller is your only patient for now. My other one got moved out to the floor two hours ago. Since you were late, they shuffled the assignments."

"If anybody else comes in today, they're all mine." Lily knew the drill. In all likelihood, she'd be in charge of another patient by lunchtime. ICU was rarely dull, Mondays especially so. Her *drunk driving* experience was sure to be only the start of an adventuresome day. "All right, then. Tell me about Mr. Miller."

"He works at one of the tire recycling places around here. The tires go through a shredder there before they can go on to the next phase of processing. Only something got jammed, and he shut the machine down to search for the problem, but some trainee who'd been out back smoking a cigarette with earbuds blasting who-knows-what into his ears and drowning out the PA announcement came along and blew it all to smithereens by pushing the big red button that started the shredder back up."

"Oh, no." Lily's stomach dropped.

Lyza took a big breath and exhaled, fluffing her bangs as she did so. "Fool kid could've killed someone, but luckily the supervisor shut the machine back off within seconds. Mr. Miller's arm was decimated. He was in the OR for hours but the doctors couldn't save it. There are a lot of other contusions and bruises, but the amputation is the worst. He ended up with an SD."

Shoulder disarticulation. His arm had been removed at the shoulder joint. As often happened with patients brought into the ICU, his life was headed in a whole new direction.

Lord, help him adapt.

Lily was helping Jacie, one of the newer nurses, with a bedding change in room 4150 when the charge nurse — whose voice carried across the unit even if she whispered — yelled from the front desk. "Lily, we got a hot one coming in! Now!"

She spared a quick "Gotta run" for Jacie before peeling off her gloves and leaving Mrs. Rivera's room behind her.

"Tell me what we know." How much information they received depended greatly on where a patient came from. Sometimes the details were sketchy at best.

The charge nurse, with her short gun-metal grey hair and perpetual frown, was all business. "Female, fifty-five years old. Son found her collapsed and phoned for an ambulance. ER cites severe dehydration and ketoacidosis. She's ours until we can get her blood sugar stable."

Lily nodded. "You said hot?" That was a term they used when a patient was combative.

"Not her. The son. All they told me is that most of the emergency room emptied out as soon as he marched in."

Oh, dear. Gang banger? Giant Samoan wrestler? Covered in body art and piercings? Please don't let him have metal spikes drilled into his skull like that guy last month!

Lily took the paperwork from the charge nurse. She peeked in on Mr. Miller — no change there — before moving on to open the glass doors of Mrs. — she glanced at the papers — Graham's room for the transport team to wheel her hospital bed into place.

"Hi, Mrs. Graham. My name's Lily, and I'm going to be your nurse today. Are you comfortable? Can I get you anything?"

"No, dear, I'm fine. Everybody's making way too much fuss. I'd rather be allowed to go home."

A visual assessment of the patient showed bright eyes and good color. Her speech was clear, too. Lily made a couple notes on the chart then tugged the stethoscope from around her neck and placed its diaphragm against her hand to warm it. "I need to listen to your heart and lungs for a second. This might be cold. Try to ignore me and breathe like normal."

The rustle of movement behind her announced someone's entry, most likely the son.

"Caleb, dear, will you please say hello to Lily? She's my nurse."

She gritted her teeth behind a bright smile as she circled to greet Mrs. Graham's son, the man who had single-handedly driven everyone out of the Emergency Room. Lily ended up face-to-face with a whole lot of grey. The man wore a uniform, and not just any uniform. A quick step back allowed her to look up at his face without having to crane her neck. Her gaze raked across his unshaven jawline and grey eyes, but that wasn't where her attention landed. A well-worn cowboy hat topped his head in place of the typical state trooper's campaign hat.

A uniform and a cowboy hat both... Good thing she wasn't the type to get weak in the knees.

"Hey, Lily." Rinaldo, one of the respiratory techs, hollered to her as he approached the door. "Police are on the unit. Did they come to haul you away after your run-in this morning?" The tech popped his head over the threshold, but as he took in the scene, his eyes grew into saucers and he backpedaled out the door. Lily watched from the corner of her eye as her friend abandoned her and sped down the corridor.

"I hope you nurse in a straighter line than you drive."

That voice!

She hadn't gotten a good look at the trooper. During her sobriety test, he'd stayed between her and the cruiser, backlit the entire time. She'd been in the spotlight while he'd remained in the shadows. He would have had a clear view of her, but she'd not been able to garner much more than an impression of his appearance. His voice, though, pure velvet with the subtle hint of a Southern drawl, was unforgettable.

"You!"

Two

Caleb rubbed his eyes. The beauty from that morning stood in his mom's hospital room. He'd realized, of course, that she wore scrubs when he'd put her through the paces of the field sobriety test, but he'd figured she worked at a nursing home or in a doctor's office. With her long blond hair drawn up in a casual pony-tail-type-bun thing on her head, and her blue eyes regarding him with shock and accusation, he couldn't help but think her too delicate for the grueling work of an ICU.

"You!" She sputtered.

Okay. Not so delicate, after all.

Her cheeks bloomed bright red as her hands fisted at her sides. Those eyes of hers, so big he could go swimming in them, no longer gazed at him with apprehension as they had that morning. In fact, if he wasn't mistaken, her eyes were downright murderous.

Why was she mad? He'd let her off with a warning.

"Oh, this is wonderful! You two know each other. Caleb's lived here such a short time, and I've been worried about him making friends. Tell me how the two of you met."

Her smile looked forced as Lily filled the silence. "It was an informal introduction, really. I'm not sure you could even say…"

He swallowed the lump in his throat and cut her off. "Uh, on the job, Ma. We met on the job."

His mom eyed him speculatively. "You didn't bully her, did you?"

A groan escaping his lips, Caleb dropped into the room's only chair. "No, Ma, I didn't bully her. Why would you think that?"

"I wasn't born yesterday, son. I know an evasive answer when I hear one. Informal introduction. On the job. *Hmph.* Your job is arresting people."

Was it him, or was the temperature climbing? If only he could open a window. Lily smirked, and he resisted the urge to fan himself. The little minx was enjoying this!

She pivoted back to face his mom, thank goodness. He closed his eyes and propped his head back against the wall, hat in his hands. As soon as the ER doctor had assured him Ma would recover, his adrenaline rush had begun to ebb. Between that and the long night at work, Caleb had little motivation to do anything more than sit and listen to the conversation.

"We're going to keep you on a saline drip with some potassium in it to help you stabilize, but I need you to drink as much as you can to nudge the process along. You'll get an insulin drip, too, as soon as the pump for that gets here."

"Do I call you Lily or Nurse Lily? I'm never quite sure."

Her face was hidden from him, but he heard the smile in her words nonetheless. "You can call me Lily. I'd prefer it, in fact. I'll bring you a cup of water. Drink as much as you can."

"Of course, dear. I'll do whatever you say. I want to get well and go home again."

Lily went to fetch the water, and silence wrapped itself around Caleb. He was almost afraid to open his eyes. His mom was staring at him. He could sense it.

"You can't fool me, son. I know you're awake."

He cracked one eye.

"You need to go home and sleep. I'll be fine."

"I'm not leaving, Ma, so forget it."

Lily walked back into the room with an industrial-sized cup of water that sported a corrugated plastic straw sticking out through its lid. She rolled a table close to the bed and set the drink within easy reach of his mom. "I've been instructed to check your blood sugar every hour, too, until the readings become more consistent."

Caleb noticed the device in her hand. He hated those things.

She continued without sparing him a glance. "I fetched the unit's glucose meter, but the lancet is kind of big. We can use yours instead if you have it with you. Home models tend to use a smaller needle, which means a smaller poke."

Ma frowned. "I wasn't conscious when the ambulance came for me. I couldn't grab anything."

"I brought it." Both women turned to him, eyebrows lifted. Maybe he should be offended that they looked so surprised. Reaching beneath the chair, Caleb extracted the small overnight bag he'd brought. "I grabbed some things for you, Ma. All your prescriptions, your glucose meter, toothbrush, a fresh set of clothes for going home, and some other stuff. I don't remember what all I jammed in here, but that was one of... Aha!" He waved the small vinyl satchel in the air. It held Ma's meter plus the lancets and the test strips.

Lily didn't smile at him, but her eyes shone with approval. Either that, or he *really* needed some sleep.

She took the device with a soft "Thank you," and went about her business, checking his mom's blood sugar. "How long were you unconscious?"

"Not very long, I don't think. I remember getting up when my alarm went off. I started for the kitchen to make some coffee. The next thing I recall is being in the ER."

"Ma gets up at seven and makes it downstairs by half past. I arrived at a quarter to nine and found her."

Lily nodded. "That's not nearly as bad as it could have been, then. Imagine if nobody stopped by this morning to check on you."

"Oh, he wasn't visiting. Caleb lives with me. Moved in a couple months ago."

He cringed. Fantastic. What every woman wanted. A grown man who lived with his mother. Just in case the first impression he'd made wasn't bad enough, he got to repeat it all with a second, even less favorable impression.

Closing his eyes again, Caleb leaned his head back and decided to focus on the sound of Lily's voice. It was soothing. She had a way about her. Ma was in good hands…

"Drunk driving? He didn't!"

His mom's incredulity filtered through the veil of sleep and pulled Caleb back toward consciousness. Remaining still, he assessed the situation.

"He wasn't a tyrant, was he?"

Why did Ma always assume he went out of his way to frighten people?

"Not exactly." Lily was still in the room.

Or in the room again. How long had he been asleep?

"Just… a little intimidating."

Caleb listened to his mom's *harrumph* and waited for her to ask what he'd done wrong. He'd let her off with a warning. That had to count for something. What could she possibly be holding against him?

"Tell me what he did, and I'll talk to that boy of mine."

Lily's soft laughter filled the room. "You don't have to do that. I'm sure he doesn't even realize what he did."

"All the more reason for me to point it out to him."

Good old Ma. He might be a grown man, but that was no cause for her to stop trying to correct all his character flaws.

The petite nurse's voice still rang with humor. "Now it seems silly, but at the time, when he made me get out of my car, he stood between me and his cruiser. I never got a look at his face the way he was backlit by the headlights. It was a little disconcerting at first, but I'm a sucker for a Southern drawl. I figured no man could retain such a charming accent and end up being a crazed rapist, right?"

Caleb started two simultaneous conversations with himself. *Numbskull!* … *She likes my accent… It's a wonder she didn't take off running as soon as she got out of her car! ... So I'm charming, huh?*

Ma *tsked.* "He's not used to living up here. His dad and I moved to Virginia after he finished high school. He went off to college then went to work at a sheriff's department down south. City life is new to him. I may tease the boy about being a bully, but I'm not sure he even realizes how imposing he can be. He'd never intentionally threaten someone."

Silence settled into the room before his mom added with a chuckle, "Besides, the flashing lights should've clued you in that he was one of the good guys."

The snort that came next was all Lily. "Don't forget the siren."

"He used the siren on you? Oh, my. I'm gonna have to talk to that boy."

Caleb almost shook his head at them, but doing so would tip them off that he was awake and listening.

Something his father had said as he was growing up came back to him. *Sneaky might be educational or even entertaining, but it's still wrong.*

Some life lessons were harder to unlearn than others. With a sigh, Caleb made a big show of stretching.

"Well, there you are, sleepyhead. I told you, you should go home and get some rest."

He hoisted himself out of the chair and approached the bed, giving his mom a kiss on the forehead. "And I told you I'm not leaving. Taking care of you is my job now, and I'm not going to…" His words trailed into silence as he realized what he'd been about to say.

Ma read him like a book. "What? You're not going to fall asleep on the job?"

Lily didn't laugh outright, but she did grin as she patted his mother's hand. "Your mom is doing fine, Trooper Graham. Her blood sugar is still high, but it's coming down nice and steady, which is best. The pH of her blood is still too acidic, but it's moving in the right direction, too. She's taking her fluids in and as soon as we get her pH where it needs to be, she'll be able to eat something. You can go down to the cafeteria and get yourself some lunch, if you'd like."

"Coffee's all I need. Is there a machine around here somewhere?"

The pony-tail-bun bounced as Lily nodded. "Take a right down the hallway there, and you'll find the coffee in the third room on your left. Right past the scrub sink."

"I know where the sink is." He'd been directed there first thing when he came on the unit with Ma.

Caleb returned a few minutes later to find Ma chuckling as Lily smoothed her blanket. The two must have been enjoying a conversation — or joke — at his expense.

Lily's eyes twinkled as she turned to him. "I'm going to check on my other patient, but if your mom needs anything, hit the call button. If I'm not able to come, one of the other nurses will."

She left before Caleb could stop her.

What would he have said to her, anyway? *Your eyes are the most beautiful I've ever seen. I'm sorry for standing in the headlights. Will you run away to a small Texas town with me?*

He shook his head and turned to Ma. "Given any thought to what you want your first meal to be when you're allowed to eat again?"

"Lily already wrote down all my favorites. She's such a delightful girl."

Ma was about to reach for her cup when yelling from the next room drew Caleb's attention. He strode toward the door but stopped as several staff members ran past him, heading in the direction of the ruckus. The unintelligible words amplified in volume, and the guttural sound of agony permeated the man's ragged voice.

One of the medical staff — a doctor, maybe — started yelling into the chaos. "Hold him down! Restrain him!"

A glance at his mom told Caleb he had permission to leave her side and investigate. He stepped out into the hallway far enough to catch a glimpse of the interior of the neighboring room. People swarmed the bed like ants on a piece of chocolate. The patient they were attempting to restrain resembled a bulldog coming out on the wrong end of a fight rather than a man in need of intensive care.

"In your room!" An angry-looking woman with short grey hair yelled in his face. He took a step backward in surprise. It was all she needed. She slid the door to his mother's room closed with him inside. The sound wasn't drowned out, but it was muted. The man's horrifying roars were muffled until they sounded like a bad remix of some heavy metal song Caleb held no hope of understanding.

Caleb took a quick peek at his mom. She'd pushed her cup of water away untouched.

"You need to drink, Ma."

"I can't, hon. I'll try later. What do you think happened? It sounded like that poor man was enduring torture."

The yelling stopped, and the echo of silence surrounded them for a moment before people began speaking again, but this time in the kind of normal voices that were easily muted by the walls. The throng of staff in the hallway untangled itself. People wandered back toward their posts, heads close together as they no doubt recounted the gruesome details of what had occurred next door.

"Whatever caused it, he's in the right place. They'll see to his needs."

The words were true, but still, the man's yells would haunt Caleb's dreams for a while. It was no wonder Ma had lost her sparkle. Caleb reached into the bag he'd brought from home and pulled out a deck of cards.

Ma's eyebrow lifted. "My glucose meter and playing cards? Dare I ask what else made the cut?"

Caleb shuffled the cards. "Texas Hold 'em, War, or Go Fish?"

A couple of hands later, the door behind him slid open. He wouldn't have spared it a thought, except his mom lost all color.

"I stopped in to make sure everybody's all right in here and to say sorry for the ruckus." Strain rang through Lily's voice like the twang of an out-of-tune guitar.

Caleb spun around in his chair to see what had Ma so alarmed.

There stood Lily. Her sun-bleached hair was more down than up. Her eyes were dim. And her scrubs were smeared with blood.

Three

Lily, high on adrenaline, stared at Mrs. Graham. The older woman's face told her something was wrong, but the pieces weren't falling together quickly enough. The scene she'd just left continued to play through her mind's eye like an old film reel.

Mr. Miller had started to come to while she checked his vitals. She'd called the resident and informed her the patient was stirring. Prior to anyone's arrival, though, he woke enough to become a danger to himself. His pain must have been off the charts, with the medication in his system affecting his ability to reason. When he wouldn't stay still, she'd climbed on top of the bed to restrain him so he wouldn't tear out the stitches in his shoulder. It had been the only viable option at the time.

Awake but not fully in touch with reality, he'd appeared to be caught in some sort of nightmare. Mr. Miller had shrieked out wordless screams and bucked to dislodge her. Whether he fought the ET tube, the pain from his amputated arm, or the fear of being pinned to the bed, she couldn't tell. Not that it had mattered. She'd had no choice but to throw her full weight on him in an attempt to hold him relatively still until help arrived. Lily had never thought of herself as weak, but her tiny frame was no match for his larger and more muscled form.

The whole ordeal had lasted only a couple minutes, but she would be hurting after the adrenaline wore off. Between his one good arm, the railings of the bed, and his thrashing legs, she was certain to end up with more bruises than if she'd spent eight seconds riding a bucking bull. Not that she planned to put that to the test. Even then, the beating she'd taken was nothing compared to what her patient had gone through — was still going through.

Whether it was post-traumatic stress from his accident, residual confusion from his anesthesia, or a reaction to his meds, the end result was the same. He was a danger to himself. Lily had still been straddling her patient and trying to hold him down when a doctor behind her barked the order for lorazepam and another nurse administered it.

Mr. Miller had finally slipped back into slumber after that. She'd then had to give him a new mainline for his IV drip since the other had been ripped out during their wrestling match. She'd also instructed the respiratory tech to double-check the placement and condition of his ET tube. Then she'd tackled the task of removing the dressing from his shoulder. Several of his stitches had popped, and she'd assisted while the resident sterilized and re-stitched. After that, she'd redressed the wound.

Once Mr. Miller was at last settled, Lily had decided to stop in and check on Mrs. Graham to make sure all the noise hadn't disturbed the older woman too much.

She stood in the doorway, watching mother and son. A moment passed before it registered that they were both staring at her, faces pale and eyes wide.

Her brow wrinkled. "Is something wrong?"

Caleb rose from his seat and took her by the elbow. She wasn't used to being manhandled, not that she could actually call his gentle touch that. Even if it had been, though, the concern on his face would have prevented her from telling him so. He led her over to the bathroom door and swung it open so she caught sight of herself in the mirror.

What the blazes had she been thinking, waltzing into a patient's room like that? A fresh-from-nursing-school rookie wouldn't even make that kind of mistake.

"Oh. I… I'm sorry. I'll be back in a minute."

She was almost out the door when Mrs. Graham stopped her with a word. "Lily?"

She turned around and met the woman's gaze.

"Is that man going to be okay?"

His arm had been torn from his body by the very machine that provided his livelihood — all because of one person's idiocy. *Okay* was a relative term. "He's strong. He'll survive." She indicated the macabre stain on the front of her scrubs. "His IV came out, and some stitches got pulled. This blood isn't nearly as bad as it looks."

Mrs. Graham nodded and offered a weak smile. Lily slipped out of the room and closed the door behind her.

She headed straight to the nurse's station. "Does anybody have a spare set of scrubs I can borrow?"

Maddie glanced up from the chart she was reading. "In my locker. They'll be big on you, though."

Lily gave her a tired smile. "I've been short my whole life. I'm used to masquerading as a kid dressed up in mom's clothes whenever I'm stuck borrowing anything."

Maddie walked with her toward the locker room. "Why don't you keep an extra set here?"

"I do. I used them on my last shift and forgot to bring replacements in this morning."

Dressed in the borrowed too-big scrubs, Lily strode into Mrs. Graham's room. The woman rested peacefully. Caleb's chair was back in its place, out of the way and against the wall.

He grinned at her. "I knew you were a dainty thing, but dressed like that, you look like you couldn't be more than twelve."

It was true. Lily had rolled the pant legs up several times and had even doubled the scrubs over at the drawstring waist. The top hung on her small frame and would have revealed much more than made her comfortable with its V-neck if not for the formfitting white t-shirt she wore underneath.

She couldn't help but return his smile. "I'm not sure I know any women who like to be referred to as…" Lily accompanied her final word with air quotes. "…things."

His tanned skin hid it well, as did that scruff of a beard, but the rosy hint of color on his neck gave away Caleb's blush.

"What can I say? I'm a simple country boy at heart."

If that was what boys were like where he came from, she'd be afraid to meet a man.

"Your mom told me a little about your background, but she didn't mention where you're from. I hear the South when you talk, but I can't pinpoint a location."

Caleb stretched his legs and crossed them at the ankles. "I grew up in Tennessee, but I've lived in Texas the last decade or so. Until recently."

Lily kept her words soft as she got out the glucose meter. "What brought you all the way from Texas to our metropolis?"

His shoulders dropped the tiniest bit, and he began adjusting the watchband on his wrist.

Did people still wear watches? Obviously, but everybody in her circle checked the time on their phones.

"My dad died, and Ma was all alone. Dad would have wanted me to look after her. He wasn't old. I thought I'd be dealing with nursing homes before I ever faced a funeral. They married young, though, and she'd spent every day since fussing over him and making sure he was taken care of. She was lost without him, and... I guess I was worried about her."

Lily heard what he didn't say. He'd been lost, too.

"I'm sorry for your loss. The death of a parent is hard."

His head dipped in agreement. "I've been told losing someone suddenly is harder than a long illness where you get a chance to say goodbye and make your peace."

Lily frowned. "Those long illnesses take their toll on people, too. I think if you talked to some of the people who've lost loved ones that way, they might tell you sudden is better."

He clasped his hands in his lap. "The grass is always greener on the other side…?"

"I was at a tent revival once when I was a kid. The preacher said that when the grass is greener on the other side of the fence, check the neighbor's sewer for a leak."

Laughter burst to life in Caleb's eyes, though he kept his voice soft in deference to his mom's slumber. "Sounds like a wise man."

Lily had never seen anyone so still. Most men stuck in these hospital rooms with a loved one fidgeted, played on their phones, or made constant trips to the coffee machine. Caleb, in contrast, seemed content to simply be there for his mom.

Pulling her eyes away from him, she returned to the task at hand and used a soothing voice. "Mrs. Graham, I need to check your blood sugar. Feel free to sleep through this if you'd like. You're going to experience a little poke right about now."

The patient stirred and opened her eyes.

"Sorry about that. I'd hoped it wouldn't wake you. How are you doing?" Lily collected the sample and blotted the site with some sterile gauze before putting the test strip into the meter.

"I'm fine. Is it a little warm in here?"

"I'm not a very good judge of temperature bundled up in these scrubs the way I am. I feel like I'm ready for a snowstorm in the middle of summer." Lily walked over to the thermostat and nudged it

39

down a couple degrees. The afternoon sun hitting the curtainless windows could make the best air conditioner struggle to keep up.

Mrs. Graham shrugged. "People in the hall were talking… That man lost his arm, didn't he?"

Patients heard things in ICU. It was inevitable. Lily wished that one had been avoided, though. Mr. Miller shouldn't have woken up the way he did. Not that waking up was the actual problem. The manner in which he'd done so was what troubled her. She sidestepped a direct answer to Mrs. Graham's question. "It was a work accident."

"It's going to cost him his livelihood, isn't it?" The older woman sounded worried.

"I don't know about that, but if it does, Worker's Comp is a good stop-gap. We can help him recuperate physically, and as soon as he's able, counselors will talk to him and aid with the emotional recovery, too. Our team will do everything it can to make sure he's okay."

Caleb's inquiry came from behind her. "Doesn't he have anybody? I mean, I only passed a couple rooms on my way to the coffee, but I was surprised at how few of them had visitors."

Lily was used to the question and the answer rolled off her tongue without thought. "Not everybody can be here during the day. We get more people coming and going in the evening as people leave work, and the waiting room is packed all weekend long as people wait their turn to visit their loved ones. Most patients in ICU aren't allowed constant visitors, either. Your uniform won you some points at the front desk, or you'd be cooling your heels in the waiting room, too."

With practiced ease, Lily ejected the test strip from the glucose meter and recorded the number.

"How's her blood sugar doing?" Caleb moved fluidly to the next subject.

"Her numbers are leveling off when we need them to keep coming down." Turning back to the patient, she inquired, "What do you say to some fresh water? This one's been sitting here a while."

Mrs. Graham nodded.

Lily smiled at her and rested her hand on her patient's. "You're going to be fine. We'll get your blood sugar whipped into shape in no time. Rest easy. I'll be right back with that water."

"What about his family? Will they be here soon?" Mrs. Graham's eyes drifted to the wall between her and Mr. Miller, sadness swirling in their grey depths. "People from my church could come sit with him so he's not alone."

Halfway to the door, Lily pivoted back to face the bed. "That's kind of you to offer, but policy is family only. The ICU social worker is tracking down his wife so she can be notified. There are some hoops to jump through before her employer will let us speak with her, but our social worker is an experienced hoop-jumper. She'll find a way to let his wife know what's happened. Then I'm sure she'll get here as soon as she can."

Mrs. Graham accepted her answer but didn't seem all that satisfied with it.

Intent on getting that water, Lily pivoted again toward the door.

"Don't mind Ma. She needed a whole houseful of kids to mother, but she ended up with only me. So she vents her frustration by trying to mother the rest of the world."

Lily snorted. "I'm pretty sure you were more than enough to keep her busy from sunup till sundown."

That hadn't been out loud, had it?

"She's got you there, son." Mrs. Graham's voice chased Lily down the hall.

Yep. Of course she'd uttered the thought out loud. Oy. So much for professional detachment.

Four

Caleb couldn't tear his eyes away as Lily speed-walked down the hallway.

When he swung back toward the bed, he caught the light in his mom's eyes.

She tried to feign innocence but fell short by a mile. "You like her, don't you?"

"Ma, I hardly know her."

This time his mom snorted. "It's a miracle you know her at all, given how you started the relationship off. Sirens? What were you thinking, terrorizing a young girl like that?"

This probably wasn't the best time to tell Ma that Lily was no girl. "It's not like her car displayed a bumper sticker that said, 'I'm a nice person. Oh, and by the way, I'm going to be your mom's nurse.' For all I knew, the driver was some big burly linebacker. I didn't exactly plan it this way."

His mom clucked her tongue. "You should go home. They're going to keep me overnight."

"You can't be sure."

"Caleb, dear, listen to me. My blood sugar is too high, and it's not coming down the way they want, and my blood is still too acidic. I'll be here for one night at a minimum. Go ahead. Ask Lily when she gets back. Then promise me you'll go home and sleep. You need to be back at work in, what, six hours? Rest, or I'll be up all night worrying about you instead of getting better."

"Ma…"

"Don't argue with me, young man. I'm right, and denying it is a waste of the breath God gave you."

"Uh-hem, pardon me. I brought your water, Mrs. Graham. I didn't mean to interrupt."

Caleb stared. Lily had managed to witness every single embarrassing moment of his day.

Yep. His life was now complete.

His mom winked at him, and he swore she delighted in laying conversational land mines. Did Ma think *that* was the way to get grandchildren?

"You're fine, dear. I told Caleb you won't let me go home today. Can you make him leave? He needs to sleep. His job is dangerous, and he should be well-rested for it."

Lily set the oversized water cup on the table within reach of the bed before she circled to face him. "Your mom's right. A 24-hour hold is normal for ketoacidosis. The resident's not satisfied with the last few blood sugar readings, either, so we're going to make some adjustments to the IV. Mrs. Graham will be staying at least overnight with us. If you're going to be out on the road again tonight, chasing down hapless drivers, you ought to go home and sleep. I'll take good care of her while you're gone."

Caleb let his eyes travel from one woman to the other before capitulating. "All right, all right. I'm leaving." He picked up the dry erase marker and wrote his cell number on the board by the door. "Call if anything comes up."

"I need to go check on my other patient, but I'll be back over here in a few minutes, Mrs. Graham. In the meantime, relax and drink some water. We want your pH levels to normalize so you can enjoy some meatloaf."

Lily was gone before he could do anything about it, so Caleb bent over and kissed his mom on the forehead. "You take care and do what they say, okay? And don't hesitate to call me if you need something, or even if you don't like the night nurse."

Ma reached out and took one of his hands in both of hers. "You're a good, strong, solid man, son. Just because God hasn't shown her to you yet doesn't mean He doesn't have someone wonderful in store for you."

He bit back a smile. His mom had been saying things like that to him since his twentieth birthday. "I love you, too, Ma. I'll come by in the morning when my shift is over."

As he sauntered down the hall, Caleb caught sight of a flaxen pony-tail-bun.

Who said God hadn't shown her to him yet?

Caleb set his alarm and lay down to get some sleep before heading back in to work. His mom's words wouldn't leave him alone, though.

You're a good, strong, solid man.

Ma always told him he was too much like a country song to fit into the real world. All those lyrics about holding on, being by her side, and loving for eternity.

Maybe she was right. Either he belonged in a song, or in another era. Definitely in another state. He was never going to assimilate into the hustle, bustle, and congestion of northern Virginia. In fact, he didn't even want to.

What he'd seen of northern Virginia so far didn't impress him. Sure, there were sights to visit, museums to take in, and more culture than any person could absorb during a single lifetime. Everybody was in such a hurry, though, always rushing from one place to another. It got exhausting. Caleb figured that about eighty percent of the people he pulled over ended up blaming him for pulling them over and interrupting their schedule rather than admitting they'd done something wrong.

He folded his hands behind his head, closed his eyes, and waited for the whitewashed regret to come.

Instead of the usual stress he experienced whenever he thought about life since he'd moved to the area, though, something entirely different swirled through his midsection. On a scale of one to ten, it was somewhere between a toe tickle and a shoulder rub.

Was it... anticipation?

Sparkling blue eyes danced along the edge of his conscious thought, pushing aside his maudlin introspection about living so near the nation's capital. Only one thought remained as Caleb drifted off to sleep...

He had to find a way to run into her again.

Caleb sighed as he pulled over yet another speeder along his stretch of Lee Highway. Some nights, his job got monotonous. Those were the times his mind wandered. When he wasn't busy wishing for something more exciting to do, he longed for the wide open spaces of Texas. Other than caring for his mom, he hadn't much bothered to make a place for himself in this area he now called home. He hadn't joined a church, made friends, or met any of his new neighbors yet. For someone who was used to the friendly camaraderie of small-town Texas, the big city had not brought out the best in him.

"Unit 56483 here."

"Unit 56483, go ahead."

"I need a check on Virginia license Charlie Tango Alpha Zero Zero Niner."

"Ten-four, 56483. Give me a second."

Linda was on tonight. That was good. She was efficient and good at catching things other dispatchers sometimes missed.

"Unit 56483, give me a vehicle description."

Caleb frowned. That wasn't normal. "Four-door sedan, maroon, late model Benz."

"Backup en route, 56483. Plate Charlie Tango Alpha Zero Zero Niner reported stolen earlier this evening. Vehicle description is not a match. You are advised to remain in your cruiser until backup arrives."

There was no telling how the people in that car were equipped. He counted five heads, but that didn't tell him enough. Drunk college kids or arms dealers with armor-piercing bullets and heavy artillery — either was possible.

Before he could call back to dispatch and confirm he would wait for the cavalry, the car peeled out in front of him. Caleb flipped on his siren and grabbed the radio. "Unit 56483. Suspect fled traffic stop. In pursuit eastbound on Lee Highway almost to Haymarket."

"Ten-four, 56483. Keep vehicle in sight. Backup is on its way. Additional units have been dispatched to 234 with stinger."

Route 234 ran by Manassas Battlefield Park. What with doing their best to break the sound barrier and all, they'd be there in less than ten minutes. If the car didn't turn off somewhere before then. Or wreck. The stinger — a spike strip spread across the road and designed to impede traffic — might be their last chance to stop the fleeing vehicle before it put civilians in real danger.

The older car sped past the last turnoff into Haymarket. The next notable intersection would be University Drive.

The speeding car zipped through that light without slowing, and Caleb released a sigh. The stinger would work. "Unit 56483. Passing University. ETA to 234 under five minutes."

"Unit 56483, be advised, stinger is not in place. Repeat, stringer is not in place. Troopers are not at intersection yet."

That was near the bottom of his things-you-want-to-hear-while-in-a-high-speed-car-chase list. The only thing worse at that point would be a report of shots fired and a trooper — or any officer — down. Without anyone at 234 to stop them, the perpetrators would blow through the intersection, and it wouldn't be more than a couple minutes until they were in a densely populated area with far too many civilians at risk.

Caleb was reaching for the radio again when the fleeing car fishtailed. He braked hard and fought to maintain command of his cruiser while avoiding the now careening vehicle in front of him. The sedan lurched across the highway and came to a grinding stop in a ditch to the left of the road.

"Unit 56483 here. Suspect lost control. Vehicle is stopped on westbound side of highway on two-lane stretch between Manassas and Haymarket."

Linda's voice came back over the line. "Unit 56483, backup should be arriving from the west any second."

Flashing lights finally filled Caleb's rearview mirror right before he spun his cruiser so that his passenger side faced the sedan. He exited the driver's side door and unsnapped the holster on his weapon, keeping low behind the protection of his cruiser. The two additional troopers, each in their own assigned vehicle, maneuvered into position, flanking the suspect car and effectively blocking any traffic from interfering with their search. Caleb nodded to the men he'd met only in passing before. His service weapon was in hand, and the other troopers followed suit before they left the safety of cover and approached the stationary sedan as a team, each from a different angle.

Caleb's heart raced while everything around him slowed down. The adrenaline flooding his system put every one of his senses on high alert. Approaching an unknown suspect was always dangerous. Nothing could be taken for granted.

Caleb shouted to be heard over the idling engine and anything else going on side the car. "Show your hands! Get your hands where I can see them!"

The other troopers echoed his demand as they all closed in on the car.

Five pairs of dazed eyes stared back at them from the interior, all accompanied by hands held as high as the car would allow.

Idiot teens! They could have gotten themselves killed — or taken someone else's life — because of their recklessness.

Caleb turned in the last of the paperwork from his overnight shift. A group of teenagers high on who-knew-what had decided to steal a car and go for a joy ride. Only they'd gone and taken a car that had already been stolen and whose plates belonged to a different vehicle altogether. It took forever to book them all and notify their parents. The job was done, though, the thieves in holding until their arraignment.

Meanwhile, the car was securely locked away in impound until its owner could be contacted.

The brisk morning air welcomed Caleb as he stepped out of the station. A quick glance at his watch discouraged him from calling the hospital. He'd phoned every couple hours during the night and been informed each time that his mom was doing better.

She's my responsibility now.

That thought had felt like an anvil on his soul when he'd first realized it. The weight had lessened, though, once he'd moved in and seen the lost look of grief in his mom's eyes across the table each day. Responsibility had always fit Caleb comfortably. Sure, he missed the freedom he'd known when it had been just him, his job, and the big open space of Texas. He was doing what was right, though, and that mattered.

Traffic was brutal as he tried to gain entrance to the hospital's parking garage. He sat through ten minutes of inch-by-inch gridlock between the street and the ticket gate inside the garage's entrance.

Had to be shift change.

Caleb caught himself craning his neck to search for a silver sedan as he maneuvered through the twisting maze of the multi-tiered garage. When he took a turn too wide and was met by a blaring horn — magnified by the tight confines and the echo created by all the cement — he gave up the search and concentrated on getting to the top.

Forget finding a spot in the dungeon-like garage interior. He was better off with the open sky above him any day.

Caleb strolled at an unhurried pace as he approached ICU. He took a peek into the waiting room. A couple of people dozed while a young boy watched cartoons.

He kept his voice to a whisper. "Are you here with an adult?"

The boy pointed to a woman sleeping on one of the couches, and Caleb offered a reassuring smile to the child.

Next, Caleb came to the ICU entrance. With a tap on the buzzer, he alerted the staff to his presence. He tipped his hat to the camera as the door opened to admit him. Then he advanced down the corridor and tried to convince himself he was there only to check on his mom — which was mostly true. Was it his fault he glanced into each passing room looking for a messy blond pony-tail-bun?

"Scrub!"

Caleb's head jerked around to look at the imposing nurse waving him down.

"You have to scrub! You can't come on this unit and not scrub!"

"Sorry. I forgot."

The nurse hovered as he backtracked to the sink and put in his requisite three minutes with the disposable plastic-bristled brush.

Once he was done, she gave her approval. "Don't make me chase you down again, you hear me?"

"Yes, ma'am." Caleb refrained from saluting as she glared.

He was still chuckling as he crossed the threshold into his mom's room. "Hey, Ma, how you doin' this mornin'?"

"Did you eat breakfast yet? You shouldn't skip meals."

Stepping close, he kissed his mom on the forehead. "I can get something here. I wanted to check on you first and make sure you're doing what they tell you."

Ma smiled. "I'm fine. My blood sugar's almost back to normal, and they're taking good care of me."

"They gonna spring you from this joint soon?"

"The night nurse thought they'd discuss it at morning rounds."

Caleb dragged the chair near to the bed and sat down. "Did you realize you didn't feel good? I mean, did you have any warning you were in trouble?"

Her eyes narrowed. "You don't need to be worrying about me, son."

He returned the stare. "Humor me."

Ma's shrug was as close to subtle as she ever got. "Things seemed a little off for a couple days before. I wasn't quite myself, but I couldn't say what was wrong. If I'd recognized how bad it was, I would have made an appointment with the doctor."

"Are you checking your blood sugar regular like you're supposed to?"

His mom averted her eyes, and he had his answer.

"Ma, you gotta look after yourself. You understand how important it is to check your sugars, right?"

The door slid open and Lily entered like a breath of fresh spring air. She was as enchanting in person as she'd been in his dreams the afternoon before.

No one who dealt with life and death every day should be that good looking.

He moved his chair back to the wall and gave her plenty of room to maneuver around the bed.

"It's not life and death."

"Huh?" Lily and his mom stared at him, confusion on their faces.

Caleb rotated his shoulders to work out the kinks. "When I pulled you over. You claimed you'd be late to your job, and I told you it wasn't life or death. Then here you were, responsible for Ma's life."

Ma shook her head. "You didn't."

Lily shrugged. "I muttered about that the rest of the way to the hospital. Then I arrived, got busy, and forgot all about it. I'm surprised you remember."

Caleb stretched out his legs and crossed his arms. "I just remembered."

Ma rolled her eyes, and he couldn't blame her one bit. He'd earned it this time with his astounding ability to make a first impression.

Lily tried to hide her smile by turning back to the bed. Speaking to his mom, she speculated, "He probably always said, 'At least it can't get any worse than this,' when he was little, didn't he?"

It was good to hear his mom laugh. He'd attempted to bring some levity into her life since Dad's death, but Caleb did intensity a whole lot better than he did lighthearted.

Five

Lily focused on the task at hand and did her best to ignore her own pulse.

A man could be too handsome for his own good without being a good man, and she wasn't sure yet about Mrs. Graham's state trooper son.

She bit her bottom lip and concentrated on checking her patient's blood sugar.

"You seem worried, dear. Is something wrong?" A kindly smile softened the older woman's features.

"Everything's good. Did you decide what you'd like for breakfast now that we're going to let you eat?"

"An omelet, please. Cheese is fine."

"I wondered…" Caleb's vowels, normally stretched a half-beat longer by his Southern drawl, lasted even longer. Fatigue marked itself in lines around his eyes. "Is it normal to admit someone to ICU for high blood sugar?"

Lily afforded him a quick nod. "The final decision is made by the admitting doctor, but given your mom's age, the extreme high of her first glucose reading, and the complication of dehydration, it's pretty standard. And keep in mind, she had a lot more than just high blood sugar. Ketoacidosis should never be taken lightly."

He nodded his satisfaction with her answer, then rested his head back and closed his eyes.

No less impressed than yesterday, Lily continued to marvel at his stillness. Not many men were so completely content with themselves. It was refreshing and... unsettling. Something about him threw her off-kilter. He wasn't the first good-looking family member she'd ever dealt with, so why did he mess with her equilibrium?

She pondered the options.

No. It wasn't his looks. It was that inner quiet of his. Could peace be magnetic?

The charge nurse stopped at the door. "Lily, can I speak to you for a minute?"

She took a quick step across the room and out into the corridor, sliding Mrs. Graham's door closed behind her. "What's up?"

"We keep getting calls about your other patient. Media, complete strangers, and more. I thought I should warn you so you don't get caught unaware."

She acknowledged the warning. "His wife's the only one authorized to receive information about him, right?"

A frown tugged down the corners of the charge nurse's mouth even more than usual. "She's a flight attendant and was on an overseas assignment.

The airline made us wait until the plane landed before allowing us access to her."

"Okay. Have we had security issues?"

The charge nurse growled before answering. "We've chased a couple people away from his room. Reporters staked out the waiting room and propositioned family members of people in ICU, promising money for photos of him. The whole floor's locked down now. Security tells me no one from the media will be getting up here, but that doesn't mean they're not going to be approaching people in the lobby or parking garage. Not even the staff has escaped suspicion. If any photos of that man are leaked, he and his wife will have grounds for a lawsuit against this hospital. A lot of jobs will be at risk if that happens."

Lily checked on Mr. Miller, who remained sedated and noncombative. Mrs. Miller needed to arrive. She could help keep him calm so he didn't hurt himself while they brought him fully out of sedation.

The dining cart met her in the hallway, and she collected Mrs. Graham's breakfast.

Breezing through the door, Lily delivered the tray. "You have an omelet here, as well as some turkey bacon, oatmeal if you want it, an orange, milk, and coffee. I went ahead and ordered you more than you requested, but don't feel you have to eat it all. A little variety will do you good, but my feelings won't be hurt if you leave food on your plate."

Caleb, who had been standing by the bed chatting with his mom, retreated to his chair against the wall. "Is everything all right out there?"

Lily glanced at him. The intensity in his eyes reached out and stilled her motion. "Of course."

"That nurse seemed to think something was urgent."

She gave him a reassuring nod as understanding dawned. "We're having an issue that's prompted more security on the floor, but it shouldn't impact your mom."

"Oh, dear." Mrs. Graham's hands fluttered above her blanket. "I hope everything's going to be all right."

Caleb glanced out the glass sliding door to the corridor, then back at Lily. "High-profile patient or high-profile incident?"

"I can't discuss it." She frowned at him. "There's no cause for alarm, though."

A brisk nod and knowing eyes met Lily's gaze. "So why didn't you tell me off yesterday when Ma was admitted?"

The change of subject was welcome, but did he have to pick that one?

She spun away from him and back toward her patient. "Do you need anything else? Would you like some more water?"

"I'm fine. I'll just eat my breakfast. Thank you, dear."

Side-stepping the chair, Lily made her way toward the door.

"Not gonna answer me?"

She angled back in time to catch the mirth lighting Caleb's eyes.

"Your mom is my patient and my priority. I'm fairly certain telling off the patient's son is in the nurse no-no book." In any event, everything she'd wanted to say to the officer who'd accused her of drunk driving had disappeared from her head the second she'd gotten her first good look at him.

"You were nicer than I would have been."

Lily grinned. "You caught me on a good day."

A summoning wave from the nurse's station met her as she stepped into the hallway.

"What's up?"

The charge nurse answered without preamble. "Mrs. Miller's on her way to the unit. She's being escorted by security. Dr. Matsui is waiting in the conference room."

She did another quick check on Mr. Miller, recorded all his vitals, and printed out the most recent chart data to take with her.

"Lily." Dr. Matsui bowed his head to her when she entered.

She took a seat and made sure her notes were in order in case the doctor called on her for any information during the meeting.

As security showed a harried Mrs. Miller into the conference room, only one thought crossed Lily's mind. *That poor woman.*

The patient's wife looked like sleep hadn't visited her in days. Dark circles under red eyes, a solid case of the sniffles, and unsteady hands gave testimony to her fatigue.

"Why are we in here? I want to see my husband." Despite her distraught appearance, Mrs. Miller commanded attention.

"We thought it best to explain your husband's situation to you first and prepare you for what to expect." Dr. Matsui was calm, his voice soothing.

"No." The woman apparently didn't want to be soothed. "Let me see my husband. Then we can sit down and you can tell me what's going on."

"I'm not sure that's best…"

"He lost his arm. I get it." Mrs. Miller cut off the doctor. "Let me see with my own two eyes that he's breathing, that he's still al…" Her words broke off, and she stretched her hand out toward a nearby box of tissue.

Mr. Miller's wife fought hysteria. It might not be visible to the untrained eye, but the way she kept repeating the same phrase was a tell. They could either let her have her way or fight her on it and push her over the edge in the process.

Dr. Matsui gave Lily a brief nod. She tucked her charts under her arm as she stood. "Did you scrub in when you arrived on the unit, Mrs. Miller?"

The woman stared blankly at her.

Lily strove for a comforting tone. "I can take you to your husband, but you need to scrub in first. It's policy to protect our patients — Mr. Miller included — against infection."

Mrs. Miller nodded and stood stiffly to her feet. "Lead the way."

They approached Mr. Miller's door, and his wife pushed past Lily to get into the room. Once there, her momentum faltered. Halting steps brought her to the bed where she stood, hands fisted at her sides, as she stared at her husband. Then, in a flurry of motion, her hands went everywhere at once. One second she gripped his remaining hand. The next, she smoothed the hair from his forehead.

Any comforting words Lily might have offered — *Don't let the medical equipment scare you* — died on her lips.

Uncertainty and fear stood no chance against Mrs. Miller's love for the man in the bed. She ran her hands over every part of him, touching every bit of skin she could find. When she was done, she rested her hand on his chest right over his beating heart while she leaned in and kissed him near the corner of his eye.

"Everything is going to be fine, baby. I'm here now." Her tone was once again strong and confident. Despite that, tears coursed down her cheeks.

Lily stood by quietly. No words would make the woman's grief easier to bear, not yet.

Mrs. Miller peered up at her. "Is he going to be okay?"

"Dr. Matsui would prefer to be the one to talk to you about your husband's condition."

Most people would have been dissuaded by her words, but not Mrs. Miller. The woman impaled Lily with her eyes. "I'll listen to the doctor, but tell me what you think first."

Lily nibbled at her bottom lip. The woman had a right to her questions, but she couldn't contradict anything Dr. Matsui might say.

"He lost his arm. That's going to require some major lifestyle adjustments. Technically, I suppose it could be called a disability. It's not an illness, though. Neither is it a disease."

"Brain damage?"

Mrs. Miller had likely seen her husband's place of employment. She understood the sheer brutality of the machine that had taken his arm and realized what a miracle it was that any part of her husband remained intact. If the shredder had been allowed to run even five seconds longer, Mrs. Miller would be a widow.

Those critical seconds that determined the difference between life and death didn't always occur in ICU or OR. This time they'd occurred at a tire recycling plant.

Lily shook her head. "Not that we've been able to ascertain, but the neurologist will need to evaluate him once he's conscious."

Mrs. Miller gave him another kiss then backed away from his bed and plucked some tissue from a nearby box. After she blew her nose, new resolve strengthened her spine and put steel in her words. "I was afraid there was something they weren't telling me. I just needed to… to see him for myself. I'm ready to talk to the doctor now."

Seeing her husband had revitalized her. Mrs. Miller was calmer than before. Her posture was more relaxed, her voice wasn't as tight, and the worry lines on her forehead had smoothed out. It was as though she'd undergone a reboot.

Lily ushered her back toward the conference room. As she did so, she caught a glimpse of Caleb watching her from his mom's room, his expression somber.

Six

Lily led a woman down the hall. The neighboring door slid open and closed again.

Probably the wife. Caleb hoped she was strong enough to stand by him. Her husband needed her now more than ever.

"How's she look?"

He glanced over at his mom.

"The wife. How's she look?"

Families often fell apart following a trauma. It wasn't pretty, but it was a fact of life.

"Worried but resilient."

Rural Texas didn't offer a lot in the way of mass murders or horrific accidents, at least not while he'd been with the sheriff's department. Caleb had seen enough to understand a few things, though. Families needed to decide from the get-go to back each other up no matter what. Otherwise, it wouldn't take much to pull them apart. And that woman and her husband were family.

Lord, please let this trial they're facing bring them closer together. Fill them with courage and tenacity.

An hour passed before Lily came back into Ma's room, peace shining in those stunning blue eyes of hers. He'd bet anything that the woman visiting next door had something to do with that.

"Good news, Mrs. Graham! The doctor said you can go home today."

Caleb's mom smiled. "I was hoping, but I didn't want to jinx it by asking."

Lily did one last check on her patient's blood sugar and charted the results. "I'm going to be tied up with another patient for the rest of the afternoon, so one of the other nurses is going to handle your discharge."

Ma's smile lost some of its usual luster. "Oh, dear. Will I see you again?"

"I'll try to pop back over to send you off, but if I can't, remember what I said. I don't want you back in here." Lily patted his mom's hand. "Check your blood sugar regularly and contact your doctor immediately if anything's amiss."

She circled to face Caleb, and his mouth got as dry as a Texas tumbleweed.

"Do you have any questions for me?"

What would she say if he asked her out?

"Um, yeah." He scrambled for something intelligent to ask. "She's in ICU. Is it normal for her to go home so soon?"

Lily's blonde pony-tail-bun bobbed with the affirmative nod of her head. "Our job here is to make people well enough to leave. We would send her out to the floor for another day if she lived alone, but since you'll be around to keep an eye on her, the doctor believes she'll be fine. Do you have any concerns? If there's reason to think she should stay in the hospital, now's the time to speak up."

She sure was in a hurry to rid herself of them.

Caleb shook his head. "No. I, uh, only wanted to make sure."

"Okay, then. I wish you both all the best, and Mrs. Graham?"

"Hm?"

"Be sure to keep this boy of yours in line." Lily's laughter floated back at them as she slipped out the door and slid it closed behind her.

He sighed.

Ma gave him her patented don't-make-me-spell-it-out-for-you stare. "You have her number, you know."

When he didn't say anything, she rolled her eyes. "You gave her a ticket. Surely you collected her contact information."

He wasn't ever going to get any peace, was he?

"Unless that's against policy or something." Ma folded her arms.

Caleb closed his eyes and pinched the bridge of his nose.

"In which case you'll simply have to pull her over again."

She had him there.

Caleb listened attentively as the scary-looking nurse with the grey hair gave his mom instructions. He paid attention as Ma signed form after form. Everyone in the room had his undivided attention…

"Mr. Graham!"

Startled, Caleb jumped out of his chair. "What?"

The charge nurse glared at him. "You fell asleep."

"Don't pay him no never-mind." His mom to the rescue. "He worked all night. He should be in bed sleeping now. Can we move this along?"

If he wasn't mistaken, the drill sergeant nurse winked at him before turning back to Ma.

That wasn't a wink… was it? Of course not. But if it was, what did it mean? Wink as in, *I understand working nights.* Or wink as in, *Hey, sexy, give me a call.*

Caleb shuddered. He needed to avoid any and all confusing winks, and if that meant staying awake, then by golly, he would stay awake.

Thirty minutes, a stack of paperwork, and three cups of coffee later, a technician was summoned to push the wheelchair down to the lobby. Caleb had apparently been judged wheelchair impaired — or it was hospital policy. One or the other. Either way, he ran ahead to retrieve his truck so he could meet his mom at the entrance.

After she was settled on the front seat, Ma leaned her head against the headrest. "I don't want to go through all this again."

"That's a plan I can get on board with."

"Your dad always reminded me to check my blood sugar. I guess without his nagging, I forgot."

Caleb's breath caught. He missed his dad and always would, but he couldn't imagine the weight of loss and loneliness his mom had to be experiencing. They had been married so long they'd become one person.

"I can nag if you want, Ma."

She gave him a weak smile. "Lily suggested I put a chart on the fridge where I record my blood sugar each time I test it. One glance, and you'll be able to see if I forgot. That way you only need to remind me once in a while instead of always being on my case about it."

He dipped his head in agreement. "That sounds like a good idea."

His mom chortled. "She swore it would save our relationship."

"How so?"

"Lily figured if you constantly hounded me about my blood sugar, I'd be as liable to take you out with a frying pan as I would be to hug you. She's right. It was one thing coming from your dad, but I'm not sure I'd take too kindly to your constant badgering."

He wasn't sure he understood, but as long as his mom knew what she was talking about, he was fine with it. "Whatever you think will work. You gonna make the chart?"

Her nod was visible from the corner of his eye as he maneuvered onto the main road and headed away from the hospital. "She gave me a website that specializes in making the charts. I can enter the information, and they put it together for me. What my sugar should be, what times of day I plan to check it, those sorts of things. Then I can print a new one out each month."

"You had quite a nurse."

His mom smiled knowingly. "She's a believer, you know."

Heat climbed Caleb's neck. "Stop trying to set me up, Ma."

"I want you to be happy."

"No, you don't. You just want a daughter-in-law and grandbabies."

"I've never made any secret about wanting those things. I want you to be happy, too, though. Can't have you divorcing my daughter-in-law and ripping those grandbabies out of my arms because of some custody battle." She swatted him on the shoulder in what was probably humor.

"What do you want for dinner?" Distraction was a good tool in dicey situations.

"Mexican food sounds good. What do you think?"

Caleb zipped across the lanes of traffic and steered his truck into the drive-thru of a Mexican fast food restaurant.

"This scarcely counts as Mexican, son."

"They serve tacos. What more do you want?"

"This is fast food. That's not the same thing and you know it."

He grinned at her. "Yeah, but I need to catch some shut-eye, so this is as good as it's getting. Now, what do you want me to order for you?"

She rolled her eyes as she rattled off a list of her favorite items.

That evening, when Caleb arrived at the station, he paused briefly at one of the communal desks shared by the patrolling troopers. His fingers rested lightly on the keyboard as he thought about looking up Lily's information. Then he shook his head and walked away.

He was supposed to be off tonight and had come in for one reason only. The captain wanted to see him, and he couldn't ignore her summons.

Caleb tapped on the captain's door and entered when she signaled for him to enter.

"Cap'n," he murmured with a nod.

"Sit, Graham."

He settled his frame into the uncomfortable chair as he'd been instructed and waited.

He'd received plenty of warnings about her. Captain Margaret Browning, one of the first female captains in the area. Whether or not she came by the position honestly was hotly debated in the locker room. No matter how she'd gotten into it, though, she'd demonstrated her capability and proven herself as shrewd as any of her male counterparts.

Nonetheless, more than one trooper had warned him. She was a terror if you got on her bad side. Caleb accepted the directive as fortuitous. Even if she intended to read him the riot act about something, getting closer to her would serve him well.

The captain sat back in her chair, steepled her fingers, and examined him.

He returned the favor.

Her hair was shoulder-length. It still boasted a few tenacious strands of brown but was mostly grey. She wore glasses, but he'd wondered more than once if they were for effect rather than need. The shiny silver frames held lenses tinted enough to mask her eyes. Without eye contact, it was hard to know what a person thought... and hard to trust them.

"Any idea what caused that car to wreck on your last shift? The one you chased?"

Caleb swallowed. "The road's rough through that area. Either they hit a bad spot that sent them lurching, or they tried to avoid a rut and overcorrected. Those are my best guesses, but I'm not an accident tech. I can say with confidence, though, that had they been going the speed limit, they would have been better able to maintain control of the vehicle."

She nodded and thumbed through some papers on her desk.

His report.

"Do you understand the implications here?"

He stared. "Joy-riding, car-thieving teenagers are dangerous?"

Her mouth tightened into a severe line. "I've been trying to convince the transportation chief to resurface that stretch of road for two years. They keep patching it, but the patches don't hold past the first snow of the season. The plows come through and rip everything up. Then they do a poor patch job and we end up with bumps and ruts all over the place."

Since when did captains care about the surface of a road?

"Two troopers have been injured in chases on that road because of the potholes. That's in the last year. The chief is a… well, the word I want to use isn't very ladylike, so I'll refrain. He has it in for me, and he won't do a proper resurface of the road because I'm the one demanding it."

Caleb kept still and listened.

"If a panel convened to discuss different transportation issues, would you be willing to testify that the shoddy road conditions caused this accident?"

"Would I be stepping into the middle of a political mess?"

The lines around her mouth tightened. "Possibly."

"You want me to swear under oath that a poorly-maintained road led to the accident and those five teens — in the midst of making a typical stupid teen mistake — could have all been killed."

"More or less."

"They stole a car. They were high on drugs. They proceeded to flee the scene after I pulled them over for speeding."

"I understand."

"But you want me to say potholes are to blame for what happened." Caleb tapped out a staccato rhythm with his foot but managed to keep the tone of his voice even.

The captain grimaced. "I'm not ordering you to whitewash what the kids did. Be honest. Just do me the favor of also being candid about how sideways this whole mess could have gone because the road's in such bad shape. That's all I'm asking. Fair treatment to both sides."

"That I can do. Tell me when and where, and I'll be there."

The hint of a victory smile disappeared as quickly as it appeared.

"Good. Thank you. You can go now."

Caleb's hand was on the doorknob when she stalled him.

"Be sure to wear your standard uniform — not dress — when the panel convenes. I'll let you know the date with as much notice as I can."

"Yes, ma'am."

Huh. Now he had more paperwork to fill out, but not for Captain Browning.

Seven

Lily stood by as Mrs. Miller, the respiratory tech, resident, Dr. Matsui, and two male technicians crowded into Mr. Miller's room. The doctor seemed to think they were better equipped than she to restrain the patient if it came to that.

Fat chance! They didn't realize how strong he was.

The doctor gave the order, and Lily stopped the drip of medication responsible for keeping the patient sedated since he'd woken unexpectedly the day before. As discussed in the conference room, everyone hoped that seeing his wife would help keep Mr. Miller sufficiently calm, allowing them to explain the situation to him. The meds could take as long as twenty minutes to clear out of his system enough for him to wake, but given his state the previous day — and his instant reaction to being awake — she anticipated it happening much sooner. She didn't peg this guy as the type to wake slowly or gently.

Her eyes on the monitors, Lily kept one hand on her patient's wrist. His pulse shook loose from its slumber and continued to increase in speed. Energy hummed through his body like an electric current. The heart rate monitor showed everyone else what she could feel, at least the facts and figures. No monitor could relay her hands-on impression, though.

"I think he's in a nightmare."

"Why do you say that?" Dr. Matsui spared her a quick glance before returning his attention to the monitor.

"I saw something similar once with a patient whose adrenal gland was on overdrive." Lily glanced at the doctor. "The second Mr. Miller's pulse sped up, all his muscles tensed. When he comes to, he's going to be fighting, like yesterday." The IV in Mr. Miller's arm started to back up. His muscles were so tightly clenched that the saline and antibiotics couldn't penetrate the muscular blockade to get into his system. What's more, blood began to seep up into the IV tubing.

Dr. Matsui concurred. "That might help explain yesterday. If he's having nightmares, he could be reliving the accident."

Mr. Miller's muscled arm twitched beneath Lily's fingers. She applied more pressure to try to hold the limb in place. They didn't want him ripping out his IVs again. She inclined her head to Mrs. Miller, who stood across the bed.

A gargled roar came from deep in the patient's throat. He jolted upright in bed. Lily threw all her weight onto his arm and shoulder, trying to keep it stationary while his wife grabbed his face with both her hands and leaned in so close that she blocked everything else from his line of sight.

"I'm here now. You're safe. I won't let anything else happen to you."

The second Mrs. Miller started talking, the tension began to ease from the patient's arm.

"I'm here, baby. You're safe, and everything's all right. I won't go anywhere. I'm right here."

His pulse stuttered its way into a slower rhythm.

"I love you, and I'm so happy to see you again. It's going to be okay. I'm here with you."

He stopped fighting the ventilator, and his breathing calmed.

Lily took over the conversation. "I'd like to let go of your arm, Mr. Miller, but I need you to keep still. Can you do that for me?"

Eyes on his wife the entire time, he gave a brief nod.

"You have an IV in this arm, and we don't want it to pull out again. That's why it's so important for you to remain calm." She eased her weight off. "We'll answer all your questions, but I'm going to tell you about some of this equipment you're hooked up to."

Mr. Miller nodded again, this time meeting her eyes.

"Can I trade sides with you?" Mrs. Miller sounded more alive than she had since arriving at the hospital, and Lily was happy to accommodate her. Careful of the IV in his arm and the tubing that still fed the central line in his femoral vein, the flight attendant stood close to the bed and clasped her husband's one remaining hand in both of her own.

Dr. Matsui sent the technicians on their way and introduced himself to the patient before backing out of the way.

Lily took her cue. "You have an endotracheal tube. You might also hear it called an ET tube. It can make you feel like you're choking, but you're not. You have my word on that. The ET tube is SOP for any patient under general anesthesia during surgery. It allows the anesthesiologist to control your oxygen levels to keep you as safe as possible. Policy here in ICU requires us to leave the tube in until we know you can breathe on your own and clear your own airway." Lily opted not to tell Mr. Miller about the complications that could occur if they removed it prematurely.

"We'll get the tube out as soon as it's safe to do so. That blue monster in the corner," she indicated the noisy ventilator with a wave of her hand, "will tell us whether you're breathing on your own or letting the machine do it for you. I know the tube is uncomfortable. There's no way around that. Instinct is going to tell you to fight it, but I need you to do your best to resist that natural reaction. Fighting the tube won't help you."

Lily went on to explain what the numbers on the monitor meant, what the central line and IV were, and which medications he was receiving. "You're stronger than most patients in here, which means you're strong enough to hurt yourself. So it's important that you follow the rules. Don't fight the ET tube. Don't thrash about in bed. Don't yank your arm with the IV." *Arm with the IV?* He only had one arm, and she'd just gone and reminded him of that.

He didn't speak — he couldn't with the tube down his throat — but Mr. Miller nodded his understanding. His eyes shone clear, the wild look from the day before and from a few moments before gone. Between the anesthesia he'd been under for surgery and the sedation since, he likely wouldn't remember any part of this day. Still, it was good to see clarity in his eyes.

Dr. Matsui stepped closer to the bed. It was time to address the patient's injury, surgery, and prognosis.

Exhaustion tugged her shoulders into a droop as Lily retrieved the lunch bag from her locker in preparation for going home.

"Tired?" Maddie, one of the other nurses, searched her face.

She stretched her neck muscles by rolling her head. "Yeah. It's been a long day."

"You think the Millers will get through this?"

"If I ever lose a limb, I hope somebody like Mrs. Miller is in my corner."

"You ever lose a limb, I'll hire a cheerleader to stand in your room and keep you encouraged. Sound good?"

Lily chuckled. "Deal."

The two departed the unit together and got in the elevator.

"So how are things with you and Holden the Hottie?" Lily pressed the button for the lobby.

Maddie snorted. "Please tell me people aren't still calling him that?"

"I can't speak for other people." Lily gave her friend a cheeky grin.

Holden had been an ICU patient not that long ago. One of the newer nurses at the time mentioned what a hottie he was, and he'd been Holden the Hottie ever since.

"Things are good. We're taking it slow."

"That's good… right?"

This time Maddie shrugged. "It's not always easy, but I guess it's for the best."

"Nothing wrong with slow." Lily was a look-before-you-leap person, so slow worked for her.

"He's spent his whole life getting to know God. It's still kind of new to me."

"It's not a competition."

The elevator dinged open, and the women began the trek through the lobby and toward the parking garage.

"Yeah." Maddie frowned. "It still makes me insecure sometimes."

"You're one of the most secure people I've ever met."

Maddie waved Lily's comment away. "He's not giving up on me, and I'm not quitting on us. We'll figure it out."

"You don't sound like you're convinced about this going-slow thing."

"Some days I wish we were moving faster, but if I say anything, he cracks a joke about how he can only go so fast with a cane."

The dark cavernous space of the parking garage met them. "I'm on level four," Lily said. "What about you?"

"Two."

Lily started toward the garage's elevator, but Maddie's voice stopped her. "I only told you because you believe, too. You could, you know, pray for us."

A compliment twinkled in the midst of those words, and Lily's tired shoulders lifted in pleasure. "I will."

Lily got off the elevator and trudged toward her car. The silence of her nurse's shoes made the parking garage eerie, almost as if she wasn't even there. It would have made a perfect scene for some horror flick.

The echo of footfalls — more than just hers — bounced off the walls. She stole a look behind her but didn't catch sight of anybody.

Hm. The sound must have carried from another level. Shift change meant lots of people walking to their cars. Of course, she seemed to be the only one parked on that level…

Lily turned the last corner and spotted her little silver sedan straight ahead. As always, she clutched her keys fisted in her hand, ready to use them as a weapon if attacked. Not that she'd ever been attacked, but it was a habit she'd developed years ago after a college self-defense course.

The dim parking garage lights reflected off the occasional oil spot on the ground, mesmerizing Lily as she walked along. When she realized she was staring wide-eyed, she shook her head to clear it.

The sleep that awaited her once she got home would be bliss.

The blast of a horn gave her a jolt. Many drivers had a habit of tapping their horn as they rounded the garage's corners to alert oncoming traffic of their approach. Sound echoed in the garage and

Heather Gray

made it almost impossible to tell where it originated. Even so, the honking had never bothered her before.

Why was she so jumpy? Hopefully a good night's sleep would put everything back in order.

Lily was feet away from her car when a shadow moved, causing her to drop her keys.

A fat lot of good they would do defending her if she couldn't even keep them in her hand!

Sure she was overreacting, Lily reached for the keys and didn't spare a second glance for where she'd seen the movement. Before she got her fingers through the keyring, though, a pair of work boots moved into her line of sight.

She shot to her feet and backed away. The man followed, getting closer than anybody's personal bubble would ever allow. He reeked of alcohol and grease. His bloodshot eyes and hair-in-need-of-washing only served to emphasize the dirt-encrusted state of his clothing.

"Wh-who are you?" Lily took another step back, but he mirrored her movement.

"I need to know how Ken is."

"K-ken?"

"Yeah, Ken Miller. You're his nurse, right?"

She eyed the panic button on her keyring. The man stood between her and the keys now, and there was no easy way around him. Even if she got to them and hit the bright red button, would anybody hear her alarm? Would they come?

"Where did you hear that?" Keep him talking. If he was talking, he was less likely to do other unspeakable things.

"It don't matter."

Think, Lily! Think! "Are you a reporter?"

Unless he was with some underground e-zine, the man wasn't media, but she needed some time to figure out what to do.

He snorted. "Tell me if he's gonna be okay."

"I can't talk about patients. I could lose my job."

"Yeah, well, I already lost mine. Now tell me about Ken."

The puzzle pieces fell together and she took another step back. A quick glance around told her nobody was coming to her rescue. Not another soul was in sight.

"You're the man who pushed the button on the machine, aren't you?"

He grunted and spit on the cement. "Tell me how Ken is, and tell me now."

IGHT

The sun faded toward the west as Caleb settled back into his truck, his meeting with the captain behind him. He needed some sleep. Leaving the station's parking lot, he swung right onto the highway and started toward his mom's home.

Would he ever think of it as his home?

His choices weighed on him. He'd done the right thing by coming to live with his mom. From a generation where people married young, she'd never been alone in her life.

She needed him. The trip to the hospital proved that.

Still… he didn't feel at home. That's what it boiled down to. He hadn't made it his home yet.

Caleb crested a rise and caught a last glimpse of the sky's brilliant colors before they morphed into the starless blanket of night.

Living in the city meant sunrises were difficult to enjoy and sunsets were almost impossible to catch. The stars remained hidden from view, too. Not for the first time, he wondered what the sunrise looked like from heaven. Man, that had to be some sight. One his father got to revel in every day.

A sense of foreboding drifted in on the evening breeze and settled into the cab of Caleb's truck, curling its tentacles around his bones and sending a chill through his blood.

The incongruity of dread so closely chasing thoughts of heaven froze him. When his mind started moving again, though, it took off at lightning speed.

He'd experienced this heavy feeling before, almost always right before disaster struck or something went terribly wrong. Heeding the warning had saved him and his fellow deputies a heap of trouble more than once back in Texas.

So who was in danger now?

The last time he'd felt it…

He picked up his phone and dialed his mom's number.

"What is it, son? You checked up on me thirty minutes ago."

"Anything going on at the house, Ma?"

"The house is locked up tight, I'm fine, and the television is keeping me company. Why?"

Caleb wasn't sure how to answer the question. "I got this feeling."

She was quiet for a second. "You call it a feeling, I call it the Holy Spirit. Either way, if the Spirit's talking, you need to listen."

The breeze shifted and the weight in his chest changed. Like an image breaking down into individual pixels and reforming itself into something wholly new and distinctly recognizable, a face came into focus.

"It's Lily."

Ma's intake of breath was audible. "Oh, dear. Did you jot down her number while you were at the station?"

"No. It wouldn't have been right."

"Then what do you plan to do?"

"I'll figure something out." Caleb came to an intersection and made a quick U-turn on the wide boulevard. "Keep your phone close so you can reach me if anything comes up."

"Sure thing. Be safe."

"Always am." He hung up, certain Ma was already praying for him. Caleb knew it the way he knew she'd leave her bedroom door open so she could hear him when he got home. Some things never changed.

Caleb eyed the clock on his dashboard as he struggled through the evening traffic. Shift change for the nurses was at seven. It was half past that, and he was forty-five minutes from the hospital.

He should have asked for her number when he'd had the chance.

Sometimes nurses ran late, though, and not just because they'd been pulled over for drunk driving.

Maybe the night nurse was behind schedule and Lily hadn't left yet.

At least he could describe her vehicle.

Never mind that he had no clue where she normally parked.

Glad he'd programmed the number in when Ma was admitted, he told his phone to call the ICU.

"Intensive Care, can I help you?" He recognized the voice from the times he'd called during the night to check on Ma.

"This is Caleb Graham. My mom was discharged earlier today. I wondered if her nurse is still around."

"Sorry, Mr. Graham. Lily's gone home for the night, but I'd be happy to take a message to give her next time she's on shift."

"Which parking garage does she use?"

"Uh…" Hesitation crept into the conversation. He could imagine her scribbling a note to someone nearby. *Lily has a stalker.* "I don't think I can tell you that."

"Can you connect me to security, then?" This was taking too much time.

"Is Lily in danger? Is something wrong?"

Caleb expelled a breath. "She might be, and I want to ask security to sweep whichever garage she usually parks in." *Danger* was a bit of a stretch, but the nurse on the other end of the phone didn't need to be told that.

The woman sighed. "I shouldn't be telling you this, but she's usually in E, the one by the main entrance. The bottom two levels are reserved for staff, but they fill up fast. If she didn't find a spot there, she would have kept going up the ramp to search for a space. Whenever E's full, she goes over to R, the garage by radiology."

Relief pushed back at Caleb's worry. "Thank you."

Caleb sped around the corner. Flashing blue lights reflected from somewhere inside the parking garage, level four or five most likely. It was hard to tell with the way the lights bounced off the interior of the cement structure. Unlike his last time coming to the hospital, he faced no delay getting through the entrance. He collected his ticket from the machine and began the mechanical motion of climbing up the ramps within the garage. Right turn, drive, right turn, drive, right turn, drive…

As he made the turn onto level 4, he came to a stop. The path was blocked by two police cars and a hospital security car.

If you could call it that.

The word *car* required a bit of imagination where the security vehicle was concerned. It was larger than a golf cart, which was a bonus, but legal on a real street? Probably not. Then again, the hospital didn't plan for high-speed chases, either.

Caleb jumped out of his truck and ran into the melee. Badge in hand, he flashed it as he came around the first car. His eyes searched everywhere until they found her.

Lily.

Ignoring the security guard approaching him, he went straight to her. She sat, legs tucked up beneath her as though trying to fold in on herself. She faced out the open door of a squad car's backseat, but she was in a daze, her stare halfway to blank.

He squatted down in front of her. Every part of him wanted to pull her into a breath-stealing hug, but he held back. Caleb still didn't have the whole picture, and it would break his heart clean in two if he spooked her and she turned fear-filled eyes on him.

He hadn't known her long enough to care as much as he did. And yet...

"Lily?"

She peered up at him. Her eyes were wide, the kind of wide you find on someone who's so tired they can't think straight but is forcing themselves to stay awake. Her hair was tumbled from its bun position and hung down her back in a loose ponytail. Her lips, faded to a barely-there pink, matched her ashen face.

"Lily, are you okay?"

She nodded and rubbed her eyes. "Are you the one who notified security?"

Caleb tipped his hat in answer.

"How did you know anything was wrong?"

"I had a feeling." From God, but he kept that part to himself. Just because Ma said Lily was a believer didn't mean she'd be comfortable with his prompted-by-the-Holy-Spirit explanation.

Her hand fell back down to her lap. "Do you get those often?"

He lifted a shoulder in dismissal. "Sometimes. I'm glad I got this one."

She stared at him, her eyes glassy.

"Hey! You the one who reported this?"

Caleb spun to find one of the officers approaching him. He stood and acknowledged the man. "I contacted security and motivated them to do a sweep." His badge was still in his hand, so he showed the officer. The guy examined it before waving him toward the other car.

"The perp's over here. He's not talking, though."

A glance back at Lily told him she was listening. He lowered his voice. "What did he do to her?"

The officer shook his head. "He chatted her up, best as we can figure, but without her permission. Doesn't seem like he assaulted her, and he didn't fight when I secured his wrists."

"Give me a second."

Caleb strode back over to the squad car he'd just left. "Lily, what can you tell me about the guy who was out here with you tonight?"

She rubbed her eyes again. "He kept asking about one of my patients. I didn't tell him anything. He knew I was his nurse, though. I think…"

Caleb reached out and took hold of her hand, pulling it away from her now-red eyes. "Ease up there. Tell me what you think."

"I think he might be the one who caused the accident. He mentioned losing his job because of it."

"I'll be right back. Then we'll get you home. Hang tight for now." Caleb squeezed her hand before setting it gently in her lap. Then he stood and moved away, working out the puzzle of Lily Ziminski.

When Caleb got to the other squad car, the back door was open. The man sitting inside couldn't be more than twenty-three and looked like he'd seen better days. His eyes held no fear. No remorse, either. His unsettling stare was simultaneously blank and intense. A chill went down Caleb's spine.

"Who told you she was his nurse?" Caleb was pretty sure he'd worked out who the patient was, even though Lily hadn't given a name.

The young man gazed at him with emotionless slate grey eyes. "It don't matter."

"It matters to me." Caleb stopped short of demanding an answer.

He shrugged. "My cousin's girlfriend knew someone who could get the name. Something like that." Another shrug dismissed the importance of the whole conversation. "My cousin owed me."

Caleb glanced at the nearby officer. "Has he been Mirandized?"

The man shook his head. "Nope, and you shouldn't be talking to him."

"Read him his rights. I need to question him."

The officer bit his lower lip and frowned. "I think you already did that, and anything he told you won't hold up in court, so you might as well call it a day. I'm still trying to figure out what went on so I can sort out this mess."

"What do you plan to charge him with?"

The officer's frown morphed into a scowl. "None of your business."

Caleb motioned the hospital's security guard closer. He'd been leaning against the hood of his environmentally-friendly work car. Once the guard was within range, Caleb crossed his arms to stop himself from poking at the man's chest to make his point. "You need to inform ICU that somebody in their unit leaked information about who Ken Miller's nurse is and that she was accosted in the parking garage because of it."

Then Caleb gave a barbed look to the officer. "Do you follow the news?"

He nodded, stubbornness in every ounce of the jerky movement.

"See anything about a guy losing his arm in an industrial accident?"

The officer turned a new shade of green as he reached up and massaged his left shoulder. "A tire shredder, right?"

Caleb hooked a thumb at the man in the backseat of the squad car. "I think you'll find he's the one who caused the accident."

The officer let out a low whistle, some of his previous bluster gone. "So, did he go after the nurse so he could figure out a way to finish the job or because he felt bad and wanted to make sure the guy was okay?"

"That's for you to determine. I'm taking her home." Caleb plucked two business cards from his wallet. He held out one to the officer and another to the guard. "Here's my contact information. Get in touch if you have any questions."

As the officer took his, Caleb held on a second longer than necessary. "I don't want to hear about him getting out on a technicality. Make sure you do your job."

A grimace met his words, but the officer at least nodded in acknowledgment.

"He didn't do anything to me. He scared me, and I got an adrenaline rush because of it, but then it wore off and I crashed, which is compounded by how tired I am from a long day at work."

Caleb glanced over at Lily before pulling onto the main highway that ran by the hospital. Her voice was slow and dreamlike, yet she still managed to talk like someone who'd done way better in science class than he ever had.

"Are you hungry?"

The corners of her mouth hinted at a smile. "Starved, but you can take me home. I don't think I want to be anywhere noisy."

Caleb meandered through the still-busy streets of the city. Cars moved around him, racing to their destinations.

"You take the no-speeding thing pretty seriously, don't you?"

"I have no reason to rush. We'll get there when we get there."

A light chuckle filled the truck and pushed away the last remnants of the foreboding from earlier in the evening. "Do you even know where *there* is?"

"I have my priorities." Caleb offered her a grin. "Food first, home after. And yes, I know right where I'm taking you. At least for the food. You'll have to tell me where home is."

The street lights shone into the cab and highlighted her frown.

"Honest. Nothing noisy. Trust me."

She sighed. "You're not giving me much of a choice, are you? My car's back at the parking garage."

He gave her hand a light squeeze then released it. "You're exhausted. It wouldn't have been safe for you to drive home."

Nine

Lily tried to stay awake but faded in and out. Caleb seemed to be driving around in circles. A lot of circles.

Hm. When had she started thinking of him by his first name? Rather than tackle that question, she went after the obvious one. "Are you sure you know where you're going?"

He glanced her way. The city lights illuminated the dim interior enough to highlight his smile.

She'd never given facial hair much thought before, but on him… it worked. What did he call it, anyway? He didn't quite have a beard, but it was more than a five o'clock shadow.

Would she ever stop being surprised at how good looking he was? Or how single-minded her brain got when she was tired?

"I'm searching for something specific, and…" Caleb's words fell into silence as he pulled over to the side of the road.

"And?"

"And I found it." One of those mobile food trucks was parked several car lengths ahead of them. Positioned in front of a bar that spat the sound of pounding bass out onto the sidewalk every time its doors opened, the truck was drawing quite a crowd.

"I'm not sure that qualifies as quiet."

"Stay here," Caleb said with a twinkle in his eyes. "I'll procure the food. Then we'll go somewhere less boisterous to eat. You allergic to anything? Is there something you don't like?"

"Nothing with nuts."

He hopped out of the truck on those words and pushed the button on his keychain to make sure it locked behind him. He jogged around the hood and onto the sidewalk. The line at the food truck was long, but he didn't seem to mind. Other people visited with each other or tapped their toes impatiently. Caleb stood by himself, his hands calmly tucked into his pockets, his feet still. The activity surrounded him but didn't touch him.

She needed to get a grip. Just because he was handsome and she'd had a thing for guys in uniform ever since she'd been in braces…

Twenty minutes passed before Caleb returned to the truck. He brought two bags with him. The aroma — somewhere between savory and downright decadent — set her taste buds to dancing.

And her stomach gave a loud rumble.

"Hungry, are you?" Turn signal engaged, he steered them back out into traffic.

"You're not taking us far, are you?"

"Ten minutes, tops. The one bag is full of drinks if you're thirsty."

Lily peeked into one of the bags and discovered canned beverages. "Couldn't make up your mind?" He'd gotten one can each of every major soda brand, plus some additional cans of diet.

The corner of Caleb's mouth tilted up. "I forgot to ask what you like, so I decided to cover all the bases. You had a rough evening. The least you deserve is a drink you can enjoy."

She popped the top on the can of lemon-flavored tea and enjoyed the wash of cool liquid soothing her parched throat. "I want to be clear. I don't ordinarily accept rides from strange people, especially ones who have pulled me over recently."

His eyebrow arched upward. "I figure we're acquainted well enough. I've seen how you drive, how you work, and how you handle stress. Besides, I wear a badge, which means I'm one of the good guys."

"Where did you go to charm school? Tennessee or Texas?"

Silent laughter shook Caleb's shoulders as he left the main road and entered a shopping center parking lot.

"I thought you promised me quiet."

"Hey, if it were up to me, we'd head out to the boonies, pull into the woods somewhere, and sit on the tailgate to eat. You're a city girl, though, and I didn't want to scare you with my countrified ways."

Caleb navigated his truck around to the back corner of the parking lot and into a spot that faced a wall of trees. He inched closer, though, and Lily understood why he'd selected that exact location. A gap in the tree line gave them a view down at a fountain lit from below. Their parking lot was elevated thanks to the uneven terrain. With a twenty foot height advantage, the view of the fountain was spectacular. The lights beneath the pool of water changed color as streams shot up into the air in different patterns.

Lily had seen the fountain before on the news. It got a lot of press during the holidays. She'd never been there in person, though. "It's beautiful."

"Not as beautiful as you, but it'll do."

Lily glanced over at her truck mate. "Flattery's not going to get you very far unless you feed me, and even then I make no guarantee."

Caleb began pulling out containers of food from the other bag. "You can choose from beef, chicken, or pork tacos, a steak burrito, some tortilla chips and *queso*, and *tres leche* for dessert."

"One, how did that all fit into a single bag? Two, you may have overestimated how much I can eat."

They weren't parked under one, but enough lights were scattered throughout the parking lot that Lily had no trouble spotting the flush that climbed Caleb's neck.

Had she embarrassed him, or was he shy around the fairer sex? He was all man, so she tossed shy to the side. She imagined women had been trying to catch his eye for years now, so he should be used to the banter. Not that she planned to catch his eye. Or even try. Curse those random thoughts.

With an intensity bordering on artistic, Caleb finished removing the food containers from their bag and arranged them on the dashboard. Then he handed her one of those plastic-coated foam plates. "Pick what you want. I also brought salsa, sour cream, and guacamole." He drew out the little plastic cups with their lids on them. "Silverwear, too."

Lily unbuckled her seatbelt and began putting food on her plate. "What's *tres leche*? Never heard of it." The burrito, still wrapped in foil, wasn't as tempting as the scrumptious-looking tacos. It was too big, too. If she ate the burrito, she wouldn't have room for tacos, and that wasn't an option.

"It means three milks. Technically, it's cake, but you won't think of it like that when you take a bite. Ever eaten flan before?"

She nodded absently as she claimed the guacamole and scooped a glob onto her plate.

"That's the closest comparison I can give you."

Once she was satisfied with the items she planned to eat, Lily turned in her seat and leaned her back against the door. "Go ahead. Fix yours. I'll wait."

Caleb didn't need a lot of prompting. He went straight for the burrito as he threw a wink her way. "Don't worry. I'll save you a bite."

When did winking become so sexy? Maybe he had an eye disorder. That was it. It was a twitch, not a wink. Twitching wasn't nearly as sexy. He had an unsexy twitch. Oh, who was she kidding? Even twitching, this guy oozed more sex appeal than anyone she'd ever met.

"Do you mind if I pray?"

Lily snapped back to reality and shook her head.

"Dear Father, thank you for keeping Lily safe tonight and for helping Ma to get better. I lift Ken Miller and his wife to you, as well as the young man responsible for the accident. Better than any of us, you understand the hurts and the hardships they're each going to deal with in the coming months. Please help them through it. I also ask that you give Lily peace of mind after her scare tonight. In Jesus' name I pray these things. Amen."

"Amen." She was touched that he'd not only remembered her in prayer, but that he'd cared enough about everyone involved to include the Millers and the man who'd accosted her. At the thought of the parking garage, though, her anxiety started to climb. She needed to alter the direction of her thoughts. She wasn't ready to revisit those events yet.

"So why aren't you married?" Worst. Change. Of. Subject. Ever. Especially since the previous conversation had only been in her head.

Caleb, who used a plastic knife and fork to saw off a two-inch section of his burrito, flashed white teeth. Was that humor or a grimace? "Surely Ma gave you the scoop."

"Mm, sort of." Lily wasn't sure she should tell him what Mrs. Graham had said on the subject.

"Let me guess." His voice was dry. "I'm not married because I'm purposefully waiting until she's too old to play with her grandchildren before I give her any."

She chuckled. "Um, not exactly. But you're close." Mrs. Graham had indeed mentioned grandchildren somewhere in between the part about her son's desire to follow God's lead and a long run-on sentence about his integrity and honor.

Caleb scooped up the part of the burrito he'd cut and moved it to Lily's plate. "Now you can try it, too. The steak's delicious."

"Thank you." She picked up a taco and asked, "So why aren't you married? Is there something wrong with you?"

He couldn't maneuver as effortlessly behind the steering wheel as she could in the passenger seat, but he managed to wedge his back against the door and look at her. "I've been praying for a wife for almost a decade, but God hasn't seen fit to give me one yet."

A good-looking man who talked about marriage as if it was desirable. Sexy just went to a whole new level of dangerous.

"In all that time you haven't received any offers?"

Color crept up his neck again. "A few, but I'm not sure I'd count the drunk women who proposition me to try to avoid a ticket."

It was Lily's turn to blush. Heat climbed her chest, and she hoped the matching flush stopped its ascent before becoming visible.

Between bites of his burrito, Caleb told her, "The older I get, the more I want marriage, but God's had different plans. Who knows? Had I been married with a passel of kids when Dad died, I might not've been able to come up here and help out Ma. Tell me. What would have happened to her if she passed out with ketoacidosis and I wasn't around to check on her?"

"God has a purpose for everything." It wasn't exactly an answer, but Lily believed it with all her being. Even though good people — the ones who filled her heart with hope for mankind —were forced to deal with horrendous situations, often through no fault of their own, she chose to trust God's sovereignty. She didn't bother denying that it sometimes rocked her faith. She always found her footing again, but some days came and went where every conversation with God was of the single-syllable variety. *Why?*

"Not only a purpose, but a plan, too." Caleb spoke with surety. "God doesn't throw us into something and abandon us there. He's mapped a way out of the mess and confusion. We simply need to take our eyes off the obstacles and terrain to look at His map. It's so easy to get wrapped up in what's right in front of us, though, and to forget where we really ought to be turning for direction."

Lily polished off another taco and reached for a napkin. "How long have you been in Virginia?"

A terminal diagnosis couldn't have been delivered with any more cheer. "Almost four months." He took a drink of his soda. "What about you? Born and raised?"

"Divorced parents. Grew up in Chicago with my mom but visited my dad here during the summers."

"Is he still in the area?"

Lily shook her head. "Dad works in technology, and not too long after I started nursing, the bottom fell out from under the tech industry. A lot of people around here got laid off. He figured it would reach him before too much longer, so he shifted careers and ended up down south."

"Texas is south," Caleb drawled with a smile.

She finished off her tea and put the empty can back into the cup holder. "His home's in Louisiana, but he travels all along the Gulf and through the bayous. When he lived here, he worked on the machines that make microchips. Now, instead, he works on the equipment used in some kind of environmental science. He tries to explain, but I don't follow most of what he's saying."

"You want anything else?"

Glancing down, Lily realized she'd eaten all her food. "No, I'm full. I wasn't even sure I'd be able to eat it all to begin with."

Caleb took her empty plate and cleared the assorted containers off the dashboard. Then he produced two clear plastic clamshells, each with a wedge of juicy-looking cake inside. He handed one to her with a clean fork. *"Tres leche."*

She eyed the concoction dubiously. Lily wasn't one for soggy food. Unless it was soup. Sometimes even stew. His kindness was touching, though, and she didn't want her time with him to end. Proper etiquette — as proper as etiquette could be in the cab of a truck — demanded that she at least try it. With trepidation, she popped the top of the clamshell container open and used her fork to break off a small piece of the cake.

She gingerly put it in her mouth, Caleb's eyes laughing at her the whole time. Once the cake hit her tongue, flavor exploded and she found a new favorite food.

Three bites later, she finally spoke. "I admit, the idea of wet cake didn't quite do it for me, but this is delicious. How did you discover it?"

"The wife of one of the guys at the sheriff's department where I worked back in Texas — she would bring it in to the station every now and again. It was so good I started bribing her to make me some. This is the closest I've come across since moving here."

"Let me get this right. You've only been in the area four months, and you already know the best places to park, the best burritos and tacos, and the best dessert."

He nodded sheepishly.

"Yet you didn't realize Lee Highway was so pitted with potholes, ruts, and bumps that a conscientious driver might learn where they're at so she could avoid them all?"

Caleb rolled his eyes. "Are you ever going to let me hear the end of that?"

She shook her head.

"I was in a car chase out that way early this morning. The car was going over a hundred miles an hour, and in a blink it was out of control. Seems they hit a bad patch of road that sent them careening into the other lane. They might have swerved to avoid a rut. Either way, it looks like the highway's condition played a part."

Lily winced. "Was everyone okay?"

"Physically, yes. Legally, not so much. But that's a story for another day. You want to tell me about what happened tonight?"

She waited, but the anxiety didn't come. "I was a few feet away from my car when a shadow moved. I jumped and dropped my keys. I thought it was my imagination and bent over to pick them up. All of a sudden, his boots were there next to me. Once I stood, he kept stepping closer to me as he talked. Every time I backed up, he took another step…"

"Did he hurt you?"

"No. He scared me, but he didn't touch me. He might have. His eyes were so weird, like he was on drugs, but different somehow. Just when I started to panic, the security guard drove around the corner. I owe you my thanks for his perfect timing. He told me they weren't scheduled to patrol that garage for another thirty minutes."

"You were in shock when I came on the scene."

"It was a long day at work, and I hadn't eaten since lunch. Add the adrenaline crash, and I was wiped out." She swept her hand across the bags from the food truck, adding a flourish at the end. "I'm back to normal now. This was kind of you."

Caleb nodded. "You seem better. I was worried about you there for a while."

The silence settled around them as they both finished off their cake.

"Sure you're not leaving anything out?"

Add protective to the list of the man's sterling qualities.

"I'm fine. Honest."

"All right, then. Buckle up and I'll take you home."

His gaze rested on her long enough that she expected more questions. He finally turned away, though, and the tension in Lily's shoulders eased.

Caleb clicked his seatbelt into place a second before he brought the truck's engine to life. "Grab another drink out of the bag if you want. I bought plenty."

Ten

Caleb insisted on walking Lily all the way to her apartment door. Safety first and all that. It had nothing to do with not wanting to say goodnight to a particular fair-haired nurse.

"You don't have to walk me in. I'm a big girl."

"If you lived in a house, I might let you talk me into staying in my truck, but even then I'd wait till you were safely inside the front door. I can't sit in my truck and see your front door, though, so I'm coming in with you."

Her eyes snapped, telling him he wouldn't get off so easy next time. Her fatigue was probably saving him from experiencing the rebellious streak he was sure lurked beneath the surface.

Lily opened her apartment door and angled back around to Caleb before stepping through. "Thank you for the ride home. You're right. I wasn't safe to drive myself. The fountain was lovely, too. It helped me unwind."

"Happy to be of service, ma'am." He tipped his cowboy hat to her.

She rolled her eyes. "G'night."

Then the door closed, and Caleb was left standing in the hallway. He exited the building and climbed back into his truck. The jangle of bells —the ring tone he'd assigned to his mom — filled the cab.

Keys still in one hand, he answered. "What's up, Ma? Is everything all right?"

"I'm dandy. Did you find Lily?"

A quick glance at the dashboard clock told him Ma should be asleep, not calling him. "She's fine. She had a scare, but it's okay now. I'll tell you about it tomorrow."

"Oh, that's good." Then, "Where are you?"

"I dropped Lily off at her place and am heading your way as soon as I hang up."

His mom's good cheer was unmistakable. "You gave her a ride home? So you have her number now, right? Did she agree to a date?"

Caleb pinched the bridge of his nose. "I didn't think to ask for her number."

"What?" His mother had perfected the art of exasperation. "What do you mean, you didn't think to ask?"

He weighed his options. "I need to run a quick errand. I'll be home after. Get some sleep, Ma. Everything's fine."

"Son, I realize you like to do things your own way, but take my word for it. You won't ever marry the girl if you can't contact her."

"I'm losing you." Caleb raised his voice. "You must be going through a tunnel. The connection's breaking up!"

He disconnected the call and started his truck with a grin. There were only so many ways a grown son could politely escape a conversation with his mother. The tunnel was his.

Two days later, as Caleb walked into the station, he got a text. *Found your note. Thanks again for the ride.*

He smiled and typed his reply. *Anytime. Back to work yet?*

Lily answered, *Tomorrow. Picking up car tonight.*

The night he'd taken her home, Caleb had offered to give her a ride the next day so she could collect her car. She'd declined, saying she would call a friend when the time came. He might have stood a chance at changing her mind... if he'd gotten her number. As his mom continued to kindly point out, convincing Lily they were meant to be together would be difficult without a means of contacting her.

Now that she'd texted him, though, her number was tucked securely away in the storage vault of his contact list. He wouldn't tell Ma quite yet, though. He was curious about how long she'd hold her peace before bringing it up again.

His phone buzzed, and he read the text as he clocked in. *What about you? Chasing down innocent civilians tonight?*

Hopefully just the guilty ones this time.

Be safe.

Lily cared about his safety. That was all kinds of good.

Always am.

Caleb stored his gear in his locker and moved in the direction of the wall-mounted duty roster to check where he was assigned for the night. When he'd first been put on Lee Highway, he'd thought it was a dead zone and had been irritated. Being a newbie at the station was one thing, but as a newbie who'd been able to circumvent most of the standard training because of his previous law enforcement experience, he'd assumed the assignment was a kind of hazing. Time had proven him wrong, though. His regular beat was anything but quiet.

"Ready for another high-speed chase?" Sebastian, the source of the question, approached.

"Bring it on," Caleb replied good-naturedly.

He moved on to the assignment wall, and Sebastian stayed a claustrophobic half-step behind him, off to his right. Obviously the kid had missed the class about personal space. He tried to shake the annoyance off and read down the columns of assignments. When he found his name, he stopped, read it again, and peered over at his shadow. "You know anything about this?"

The younger trooper rocked on his feet. Fast. "Cap'n ordered me to ride with you for six weeks."

With the exception of training rookies, Caleb had been riding alone since he'd graduated from being one himself. The occasional ride-along was one thing, but Sebastian's eager attitude and nervous tendencies would drive him plumb crazy within the first shift. He glanced up at the captain's office. Dark. She'd gone home for the night. Great.

"Graham!"

His head snapped around to find the source of the yell. The sergeant waved him over.

"Stay here, Sebastian. I'll be back in a minute."

Not allowing the other trooper a chance to respond, Caleb jogged toward the sergeant, who handed him a phone then went back to the paperwork in front of him. Reluctance slowing his movements, Caleb put the phone to his ear. "Hello?"

"I've assigned Sebastian to ride with you for the next six weeks." The captain's tone was sharp, her words clipped.

"Why?" What had he done to tick her off?

"Look, Graham, we both know you're destined for bigger and better. You'll move up out of this station soon, either in a different branch of local law enforcement or into something federal. I'm going to take advantage in the meantime. Sebastian will be with you for six weeks."

"He's already been through his rookie orientation, hasn't he?"

Her sigh almost made him regret the question. "This is his last chance. Turn him into someone the rest of my troopers can stand to be around. Teach him everything you can, not just about the job, but about how to carry himself, how to talk to people, how to remain calm under pressure. After those six weeks, I'll rotate him out."

"And somebody else in?"

"I may be willing to negotiate."

Caleb shook his head in admiration for her tactics. "Does it occur to you that I might be perfectly happy to stay here, but that doing this could drive me to seek employment elsewhere?"

"Not for a second. You want people to be good at this job. I've seen you give advice to the rookies. You're a natural at training."

"All these troopers have gone through enough training. They shouldn't be working here otherwise." Her actions threatened to impede his real duties, but he couldn't very well tell her that.

"They have all the knowledge they need to perform adequately. Adequate only gets you so far, though. I want you to teach them what they need to know to avoid getting burned out, to protect the reputation of this station, and to make an overall good public impression. In short, I expect you to teach them the stuff not in the textbooks and training videos."

Caleb sighed. "What makes you think I'm the man for the job?"

"Instinct. It's nonnegotiable. If you want out of doing it, then train someone so well that they can step in and start working with my other problem troopers."

An order wrapped in a compliment with a nice pretty ribbon of don't-you-dare-argue — not much he could say to that.

"Is it the task in general you're opposed to, or Sebastian in particular?"

"He's, uh, a bit eager, ma'am."

The captain's laughter reached him across the phone line. "Which is why he, more than most, can benefit from this. Top of his class in every category, but he got stuck here instead of at a bigger station because people can't stand him. I want you to fix him. His future is pretty bleak otherwise."

Resignation settled into Caleb's bones. "Yes, ma'am."

"Get to know him, Graham. I think you'll find there's more to like about him than you realize. You can't deny he needs the help."

"Yes, ma'am."

"All right, then. Safe patrol tonight." The line went dead, effectively cutting him off. Not that he had anything of value to add.

Caleb glanced up and found Sebastian. The man stood right where he'd been left, watching like an eager puppy. He even waved.

Dear Lord, give me patience.

"Well, that was fun!" Sebastian's voice grated on Caleb's nerves.

"It was a ticket. Speeding. Not worth getting worked up about."

"Is it always like this on patrol? It seems like a bunch of nothing then — *bam!* — excitement."

Caleb sighed for the umpteenth time since sunset. "There's an abundance of nothing, a little bit of something, and a whole lot of being present. As a trooper, your presence alone should be enough to deter most people from doing the illegal things they might otherwise be inclined toward."

"You don't like me much, do you?" At least Sebastian was matter-of-fact, not whiny.

"I don't know you well enough to offer an opinion."

"Yeah, but I get on your nerves."

"Yes." He couldn't argue. "That you do."

"It's because I'm enthusiastic, isn't it? People tell me that all the time. I'd like to be more like you. You look like you're standing still even when you're moving, but that's not me. I can't do it."

If he let him, Caleb was sure the younger trooper could hold an entire conversation on his own.

"How do you do that? How do you stay so calm all the time? I don't do calm. I'm not good at it."

He waited, knowing Sebastian was far from done.

"Well? How?"

Caleb sighed. Again. "Don't waste your time trying to be somebody else. Take who you are and work it to your advantage."

"How do I do that?"

"I imagine most people aren't annoyed by your enthusiasm. Your constant chatter is another story. Find a way to direct your energy into something other than talking."

"Like what?"

"Give it some thought. I'm sure you can think of something." An idea sank its tentacles into Caleb's mind. "Why don't you not speak for five minutes? Spend the time thinking about other ways you can channel all your zeal."

Sebastian rolled his eyes. "I'm a little old for the quiet game, don't you think?"

"No game." He called their location in to dispatch before continuing. "Talking and listening can't happen at the same time. You ought to know that by now. It's as true inside your own head as it is in a classroom. You're probably full of ideas about things you could do differently, but you're so busy talking that you can't hear yourself think." For the record, Caleb couldn't hear himself, either.

A long-suffering sigh came from the passenger seat of the cruiser. "Fine. Five minutes."

"Has it been five minutes yet?"
"No."

"Now?"
"No."

"Now?"
"Not even close."

Silence filled the car, and Caleb savored every second of it. When the clock on the dash told him five minutes had elapsed, he thought about milking it for another couple, but, unfortunately, his parents had raised him to be honest. "Time's up. Tell me what you learned."

"Morse code."

Caleb coughed. "You learned Morse code in five minutes of silence with no book to teach you?"

Sebastian laughed. "Nah. That'd be crazy. I remembered that I know Morse code."

They came to the end of their patrol area, so Caleb turned the car around and headed back in the other direction.

"I have a cousin with ADHD. His doctor told him to play an imaginary piano to keep his fingers busy. Somehow it helped him concentrate. Piano's out of my league, but Morse code I can handle."

Caleb thought about asking the obvious but figured Sebastian would get around to it eventually. The wait wasn't long.

"I don't have ADHD. Not that I'm aware, at least. What you said makes sense, though. I've always had too much energy, so if I try tapping out messages in Morse code, that'll keep me busy. What do you think I should tap out?"

Everything. "Whatever you're thinking about saying out loud, tap it out instead."

"I'd never speak at all if I did that."

Somehow Caleb doubted that would ever be a genuine problem. "Maybe only say the things that still seem important after being tapped out."

"I'll give it a try, but I'm not promising anything."

One full minute of silence followed before Sebastian inquired, "You married?"

Caleb whipped his head around. "That's what you consider important?"

"I tapped it out three times, and the question's still bouncing around inside my head. All the other ones went away."

"No, not married."

"Me either. Haven't found a woman yet who can put up with me. Not sure I want that whole marriage and kids thing, though. You? Anyone special in your life? Ever think about marriage?"

The captain owed him. Big. "I figure it'd be a good thing to find a woman you can be around in complete silence. Someone you're so comfortable with that there's no need to fill the space with words."

"Or," Sebastian added, "a woman you're so comfortable with that you can say whatever's on your mind, and she'll love you anyway."

"I suppose."

The radio crackled to life. "Unit 56483, please acknowledge."

Caleb grabbed the radio. "Unit 56483 here."

"You're needed at the impound lot. Know where it is?"

"No idea."

The disembodied voice came back over the radio. "Sending it to your console."

Caleb pressed the radio's button again. "What do they need?"

Dispatch came back on the line. "Has something to do with the car from your chase a couple days ago."

"Are you Graham?" The man behind the counter brought to mind a hairless Chihuahua... having a bad hair day.

"That's me. What do you need?"

"Had me a little break-in here at the lot tonight."

"Okay." Caleb stretched out the word. "What do you need me for? This isn't my jurisdiction."

The man ran a callused hand through his shoulder-length hair. "Only three vehicles busted into, all close in description to the one you sent in earlier this week."

Caleb's pulse sped up, and his mind raced to keep pace. "Where's my car?"

"It was locked up in the back shed. The dogs smell something, but darned if I can find it."

"Drug dogs?"

The man tapped his pen on the counter. "Yep. Requested they stop by after I realized that whoever broke in had to be looking for something specific. But like I said, I can't find it. Must be no more than a trace. The folks at the crime lab don't want the car, either. They're backed up, and since the only drug found on the kids was pot, this one's not a priority. Which is fine with me, except I don't like having my impound lot broken into."

"What do you want me to do?" Caleb's interest in getting a look at the car was keen, and he hoped for an invitation.

"Hey," the guy countered, holding up his hands. "It's my lot, but I'm just a civilian contracted by the state police. Y'all provide the security and an endless supply of red tape. I don't want trouble with interdepartmental nonsense, but I thought you could give the car a once-over with me."

"Of course."

The man led them toward a back door.

"Did you notice, Graham? I was quiet the whole time. I think this Morse code thing is going to work!"

Caleb hoped Lily experienced a much more restful night than was in store for him.

Eleven

Lily whistled as she got ready for work the next morning. A friend had taken her the evening before to collect her car. A note from Caleb had been waiting under the driver-side windshield wiper.

> *I wanted to phone and ask how you were doing, but I don't have your number. Figured I'd give you mine in case you ever need to talk, or want to, for that matter. Hope you enjoyed the fountain as much as I did.*

She'd hoped to hear from him the day after the parking garage, but sunlight had come and gone without a word. The silence had been more noticeable than it should have been, given the short time she'd known him. While she'd been glad when the news reported no trooper-involved incidents, she'd still called in and checked at her own hospital to see if Caleb was a patient.

Thankfully she'd resisted the urge to contact all the other area hospitals. One was enough. More would have been downright creepy, and Lily generally prided herself on not being a creepy person.

Her face had warmed when she'd found the note, and the friend who'd given her the lift hadn't let the blush pass without comment. "Either you got a love note under your windshield wiper or a ticket. Am I seeing happy color on your face, or angry?"

Her silence had been answer enough.

Caleb's handwriting was a lot like him. Broad strokes, solid, easy to understand. No fancy curls to the letters, nothing to confuse the reader or disguise a hidden meaning. Straightforward yet somehow complex at the same time. She liked it.

Lily snuck a peek at the mirror and checked her appearance before heading out the door. Another blush met her gaze.

She needed to stop thinking about Caleb, or she'd end up with cartoon-red cheeks all day!

"Can you give me a hand?"

Lily glanced up from the chart she was reading. Jacie, one of the newer nurses, stared at her with hopeful eyes.

"Sure, what do you need?"

"Mrs. Kline's dressings need to be changed."

With a nod, Lily agreed. "Let me check on Mr. Miller real quick, and I'll be right in."

"How's he doing?" Jacie's eyes, wide pools of chocolate, reminded Lily of a scolded puppy.

"Good." She offered a reassuring smile. "They'd transfer him off the unit if not for the media.

Right now our primary focus is keeping infection at bay, handling the pain, and getting the swelling down."

A short time later, after making sure her patient didn't need anything, Lily joined Jacie in Mrs. Kline's room.

The young nurse was pale, so Lily took the no-nonsense approach. "This is a tough one."

Jacie's face contorted. Was she on the verge of crying or vomiting?

"Hold yourself together. She needs your best care, period." Sympathy would give the inexperienced nurse permission to crumble. Instead, Lily tried to push Jacie in the right direction without having to say the words.

Working as a team, the two women removed Mrs. Kline's dressings and began to bathe her delicate skin with sterile water and gauze.

"How'd she get burned so bad?" Jacie's voice was small. A quick glance told Lily the younger nurse was pale again. Her chin quivered, too.

"Is this your first time with her?"

A slight nod was all the answer she got.

Lily took a deep breath. "House fire. I have no idea if they found the cause, and how it happened doesn't change anything about how we care for her." In and of themselves, the burns weren't that bad, but they covered a significant portion of the patient's body.

"How come no one ever comes to visit her?"

Lily focused on her hands and the work they did as she answered. "Her husband and children died in the fire. I'm not sure about extended family, but our social worker should have the whole history."

They finished with the water and Jacie prepared the new dressings. "What exactly is this stuff?"

Using her forearm, Lily brushed a stray tendril of hair out of her eyes. "It's a special kind of gauze laced with petroleum jelly that's been injected with bismuth trimbromophenate."

"Huh?"

She chuckled. "Yeah, I can never remember, either. I read it off the box."

Jacie rolled her eyes. "So what's it do for her? Why do we use it?"

"Now you're talking like a nurse."

The younger woman preened under the praise.

"The gauze protects the skin without sticking to it, and the medicine in the petroleum jelly helps to fight bacteria and promote quicker healing. We use it on some burns, skin grafts, and sometimes on severe rashes and reactions. The stuff looks funny, but it does wonders. If you'd seen Mrs. Kline a week ago, you wouldn't recognize her. What you're looking at now is almost a whole new person compared to when she first came in."

"How did she end up here instead of at one of the hospitals with a burn unit?"

Lily shrugged. "I think the burn units were all full. One of our doctors evaluated her condition and determined we could treat her here. Truth be told, it's not so bad. She's going to heal. It'll take time, but she'll be okay."

"Why are they keeping her in a coma, then?"

Eyebrow on the rise, Lily fought the frown that wanted to show itself. She wasn't so old that she couldn't remember her first year in the ICU. "Did you make any of these inquiries during rounds?"

Jacie's shoulder-length hair billowed as she shook her head. "I didn't want to sound dumb."

"Ask the questions when they come up. That's how you learn."

When the younger woman said nothing else, Lily returned to the original question. "She's being kept in a coma for now. They started to bring her out of it twice, but both times her heart rate and BP spiked crazy scary high."

"Which means she's in pain." Sadness dripped from Jacie's voice.

"Probably. Anyway, they're keeping her in a medically-induced coma a bit longer to be on the safe side."

"Does anybody ever wonder if the pain she's in is physical or emotional? Maybe she realizes her family is gone, and that's the first thing she thinks of as she's coming to."

Lily again brushed the hair out of her eyes with her forearm. "You need to ask that question during rounds, Jacie. It's a good one, and one I don't have an answer for. I was never in here when they tried to wake her, so I can't say. I'd be asking the same thing if she were in my care."

"Is that what happened with Mr. Miller?"

"Yeah, kind of."

The charge nurse stuck her head in the door. "Lily, you have a phone call. A patient you recently discharged. She insists on talking to you."

Lily glanced from Jacie to the charge nurse. The woman at the door reached for the antibacterial foam. "I'll help finish up with Mrs. Kline. You go take care of your call."

"I wanted to thank you for everything you did for me while I was in the hospital." Mrs. Graham's words warmed Lily across the phone line.

"It was my pleasure. Are you checking your blood sugar regularly, like we discussed? Did you print out one of those charts I told you about?"

"I'm testing it twice each day, and the chart is up on the fridge. Caleb was especially happy about the chart. He didn't want to be forced to hound me, and I wasn't ready to put up with it gracefully if he did."

How is he? Lily swallowed the words before they spilled over.

"That's good. You stay on top of those blood sugar readings, and you'll avoid a whole mess of other problems that could come your way."

Mrs. Graham cleared her throat. "I'm hosting a barbecue at my house this week and wondered if you'd like to come."

Would Caleb be there? "What day?"

The older woman hesitated. "Wh-what day do you have off?"

Was she matchmaking? Of course she was. What did it say about Lily that she was willing to let a former patient fix her up with her grown son…? "I'm off Thursday and Friday."

"Fabulous! What do you say to Thursday, then? Around four in the afternoon?"

Who else was she inviting? The senior citizen's group? Everybody else would be at work. "I'll be there. Give me your address."

Lunch was upon her before Lily knew it. She settled in the break room with her meal and bowed her head to thank God. The swish of the door told her someone else entered the room during her brief prayer. As soon as she uttered her silent *amen*, Maddie sat down across from her.

Lily smiled at her. "How has your morning been?"

"I have a vomiter, but other than that, pretty uneventful." Maddie took a bite of her sandwich and swallowed before asking, "How're you doing? I heard about what happened in the parking garage. I can't believe we were talking right before. Are you all right?"

"I'm fine. It was scary at the time, but in the end, he didn't do anything to me."

"Was he going to hurt you?"

Lily shook her head. "It felt like it at the time, but I don't think so. He kept asking how Mr. Miller was. I don't know if it was guilt or what, but his concern seemed genuine. He sure did pick a lousy way to express it, though. I was scared spitless."

Maddie shuddered. "I'm sorry you had to go through that. I'm surprised you're still assigned to Miller, though. No conflict of interest?"

"Someone in the unit leaked the information that I was his nurse. Until they figure out who, I'm locked in during day shift. Minimizing the number of nurses he comes into contact with limits liability."

"Makes sense." Maddie finished off her sandwich. "They're insisting on a buddy system now.

We all walk out in pairs, get into one car, then drive to where the other car's parked. It's either that or security escorts you."

"Let me guess. People are making a flap."

Maddie tucked her thumbs into imaginary suspenders and flapped her elbows like wings. "Only two or three. The usual ones. Everyone else is just happy you're okay and that it didn't happen to them."

They ate in companionable silence for a few minutes. Lily polished off her apple and folded her hands in her lap. "How soon till you knew Holden was the one?"

Maddie swallowed her last spoonful of yogurt before answering. "A couple months in, I started avoiding him because it hurt too much to be near him, knowing we couldn't ever be more than friends." She wiped her mouth on a napkin. "That's when I realized how strong my feelings had grown. Why? You and the state trooper getting serious?"

Lily broke eye contact. "No. Yes. I don't know. He drove me home after the whole parking garage thing. He's a decent guy."

"Decent, huh? I heard the entire ER emptied out the morning he brought his mom in."

"He can be pretty intense. Add the uniform to that, and I think anyone who'd ever so much as stolen a paperclip from work was afraid he was there for them."

"So, not an angry sort?"

"No, but that single-minded focus he gets can be daunting."

"Hm." Maddie didn't bother hiding her laughter. "Particularly if it's directed at you?"

Lily's pocket vibrated as she walked toward the locker to store her lunch bag. She tugged the phone out and read the message.

I just got up. Ma told me about bbq. I'm glad you're coming, but I hope she didn't pressure you.

Hm. How to respond? She thought about how to respond. She did feel a bit manipulated, but she also looked forward to seeing Caleb again.

How many people did your mom invite?

The phone was silent long enough that Lily almost put it back in her locker with her other things. When it did light up, she cringed at the message's implication. *She won't answer me.*

Her fingers moved at a rapid-fire pace. *Guess we'll wait and find out. Lunch is over and phone needs to go in my locker. Hope you have a good afternoon!*

Thursday couldn't come soon enough.

Twelve

Something about the incident in the parking garage bothered Caleb, so he decided to make his way down to the jail and check on Mr. Ashton Raynott, the man who'd accosted Lily. He couldn't shake the image of the man standing by the squad car, his eyes dead.

Luckily, he'd been taken into custody late Friday, and the typical weekend delay meant he hadn't been seen by a judge yet. The guard showed Mr. Raynott into a room then nodded to Caleb, giving him permission to enter.

The prisoner stared, his eyes blank. Fish about to be dropped in the fryer had more spirit. If the man didn't care what happened to him, getting answers would be a challenge.

"I'm told you've been informed of your rights. Is that true?"

Raynott nodded.

Caleb tapped a finger on the table. "I need you to answer audibly. Have you been read your rights?"

"Yes."

"Have you requested a lawyer?"

"No."

"Do you wish to have one present while I speak to you?"

"No."

Caleb took a deep breath. This wasn't going to be easy. It never was with single-syllable answers.

"You want to tell me why you went to the hospital?"

Ashton Raynott glared at him for a whole minute before he spoke. "I wondered how Ken was doing."

"Did you intend to cause Miller's injury?"

The eyes flashed that time. "No."

"Why'd you turn the machine back on?"

"I didn't know it was supposed to be stopped."

"It was announced over the PA."

Raynott stared at his hands and mumbled something.

"It's disrespectful not to look at a person when you speak to them."

The prisoner glowered, hate burning in his eyes, but the hate wasn't directed at Caleb. "I went outside for a smoke. Had my earbuds in. Didn't hear it."

Guilt. He was drowning in guilt, and he hated himself for causing such a catastrophic accident.

Caleb ran his hand over his face and sat down across from Raynott. "Has anybody told you how he's doing?"

The dead look flooded back into the eyes.

"He's going to live."

Raynott's glare sought to incinerate him. "Right. You haven't seen what those machines can do."

"I didn't say he was fine, but he is going to live. Miller's a strong man and he's got a wife who loves him. They'll get through it together." A spark of something entered the prisoner's eyes. Maybe hope, but Caleb wasn't ready to assume too much. "How did you get his nurse's name?"

The man dropped his gaze.

Whatever he'd done, he was ashamed of it.

"I need you to tell me."

Raynott glanced back up at him. "Can I talk to her?"

Lily? Over his dead body.

"I want to tell her I'm sorry."

"She's at work."

"You got her number. Dial it, and I'll leave a message."

It was voicemail. He could always hit the button to erase it if he didn't like what the man said. "Fair enough." He took out his phone and picked her out of his contacts. Within seconds, Lily's recorded voice came over the line. He waited for the beep. "This is Caleb. I'm here with Ashton Raynott, the man who approached you in the parking garage on Friday. He'd like to say something to you."

He leaned over the table with the phone, forcing the prisoner to lean forward as well. Sweat beaded on the man's brow, but he took a deep breath and spoke. "I'm sorry about scaring you. I needed to see if Ken was okay. I didn't mean no harm — to him or to you — but nobody would tell me anything, and I thought if I caught you alone, you might tell me something. I... Anyhow, I'm sorry I scared you. I wouldn't have hurt you. I wasn't sure what else to do."

Raynott sat back in his chair, and Caleb brought the phone back to his own mouth. "Call me later."

The prisoner had no way of knowing whether or not Caleb had actually dialed anybody, let alone Lily. Except he didn't seem to doubt. Men used to lying tended to suspect others of lying, but Raynott... He appeared to trust Caleb. Which meant dishonesty wasn't natural to this guy.

"So tell me how you found out who Miller's nurse was."

The eyes dropped away again, studying the floor off to Raynott's right.

Time to change tactics. "Would you like a chaplain to visit you?"

The man snorted. "God ain't got no use for the likes of me."

Caleb smiled his first genuine smile of the day. "That's where you're wrong. God specializes in redeeming the unredeemable. Haven't you heard of the thief on the cross?"

Another snort.

"The chaplain can visit if you'd like."

The man's shoulder jerked up the slightest bit before dropping back down. "I guess it can't do no harm."

"My name's Graham." Caleb stood. "I need whoever leaked the information. When you decide you're ready to talk, find me." He slid his business card across the table, and Raynott took it.

"Sure. Whatever."

Their conversation wasn't over, but Raynott didn't need to know that yet.

Caleb drove to the vast underground parking garage. The mall it serviced bustled, full of shoppers, but way back in the corner was a small section partitioned off from the rest. Reaching the electronic barricade, he punched in his security code. The mechanical arm made no sound as it slid upward. He drove through and found a parking spot.

He got out of his truck and walked the short distance to a grey metal door where he entered a different string of numbers. The door clicked, and he opened it. He crossed the threshold and faced forward. The door closed automatically behind him. Three feet of space stood between him and the next door. A boxy black phone hung on the wall to his right, and he lifted it from its cradle. Silence met him.

"Caleb Graham here for Nick Quintaine."

A beep came over the line, and he returned the phone to its place on the wall. The next door swung wide, and a well-armed guard greeted him with a nod. "Mr. Graham. Third door on your left."

He marched down the solitary hallway until he came to the appropriate door. There hadn't been any need to frisk him. While he'd stood in that three feet of space between doors, their equipment had scanned him for firearms, explosives, and who-knew-what-else.

Caleb stepped into the room and shut the door behind him. Nick rose and welcomed him with a handshake. "So tell me how it's going."

Straight to business. That was Nick.

The two had met in college. After graduation, Caleb had taken a position with a Texas sheriff's department. Nick had gone to work for the FBI. A decade later and at his wife's suggestion, he'd taken a job with the Virginia Attorney General's office. It allowed him to be home more, be a dad to his kids, and even occasionally go on a date with the aforementioned wife.

They'd kept in touch over the years, and Nick had attended Mr. Graham's funeral. When Caleb had expressed concern about his mom being alone, his long-time friend had made a job offer. Now there they sat.

"I can't find any evidence of wrongdoing." Caleb had no reason to mince words.

"You're on a list to testify at a hearing about road conditions."

He gave an affirmative nod. "A car I chased ended up wiping out, partly because of the bad road. She asked if I'd testify to that."

"Coercion?" Nick's eyes took on a laser-like intensity.

"Within acceptable limits. Some pressure to show up and a little coaching on what to say, but no attempt to force me to change facts."

"But you agreed with her that the road was at fault."

"I agreed that it was a factor."

Nick grunted. "This would have made a better test case if you'd refused to testify or argued that the road wasn't to blame. Then we could see how she handles adversity."

Caleb tipped his chair back on two legs. "Well, now, if I had any idea why I'm investigating Browning, I might have known that."

Nick grinned. "All right, put your claws away. I kept you in the dark so you could be objective."

"If you doubt my objectivity, you shouldn't have hired me."

"Politics are king around here. I believe in you, but your findings need to stand up to scrutiny on paper, not just in my mind. That shouldn't come as a surprise. This is the big time." He snatched up a nearby can of soda and popped the top before pushing a second can across the table to Caleb. "So how's your mom doing?"

"Matchmaking."

Nick winced. "Sorry to hear that, man. It's the risk you run, living close to family."

"I'm okay with it."

Obsidian-like eyes widened. "Do tell."

"A nurse. Name's Lily."

A grin spread across Nick's face. "I know you. You wouldn't even be telling me her name unless you planned to propose. Where'd you meet her?"

It was Caleb's turn to wince. "I pulled her over."

"Ha! So on your wedding day, you'll toast me for bringing you two together, right? Face it. Without my investigation of Captain Browning, you wouldn't have any reason to be working with the state police."

Of course his friend would look at it that way. "I'll get back to you on that." Caleb nodded toward the door. "So, you ever going to tell me how you got hooked into this set-up? This place can't be run by the attorney general's office."

"I have friends in high places." Nick crossed his arms and leaned back comfortably in his chair.

"When I was with the FBI, I worked with a couple different outside agencies. Learned a few things. As soon as the governor requested I head up a sting checking into some state officials, I called in some favors and got myself a safe place to meet with my undercover investigators."

Caleb finished off his soda, then stretched out his arm and set his empty can on top of the file folder sitting in front of Nick. "Did the governor ask you to investigate the captain? That seems a little outside his purview."

Nick moved the can into the garbage and frowned. "Your investigation into Browning is spillover from another case we're handling. Always better to know if a hornet's nest is hidden in the leaves before you start shaking the tree."

Caleb wouldn't question Nick about the other investigation. He knew his friend too well to bother. Like everyone else, he would have to wait and see what the tree dropped.

Thirteen

"How is your pain level today, Mr. Miller?"

The patient studied Lily but couldn't hide his grimace.

"I can give you something for the pain, but you need to tell me how bad it is so I know which med to use."

"Bad."

His wife had gone home to shower and sleep — at her husband's insistence. The softer side he showed in his wife's presence was currently in hiding, his rough edges poking out again.

"Ibuprofen bad or morphine bad?"

Mr. Miller rolled his shoulders and his face paled. Lily strode over and rested two fingertips against his wrist so she could check his pulse. His heart wasn't racing, but it wasn't at rest, either. She snagged the blood pressure cuff from its place, but he twisted his hand around until he reversed their positions and held her wrist in his hand. "No." His grip was firm enough to border on uncomfortable. "It'll be high because I'm in pain. The doctors find out how high, and they'll want to talk about blood pressure medication. A whole new hassle will start, and my wife will worry."

Huh. Patients didn't often surprise Lily, but Mr. Miller did. He understood quite a bit more than expected, given the short time he'd been awake and aware since his amputation. "Fair enough, but tell me, are you going to suffer through the pain or take something for it?"

He'd already refused the PCA pump. It was designed to give him control of his pain meds and had a button he could push for another dose whenever he needed it. He'd refused a regular schedule of nurse-administered pain meds, too, making all their jobs more difficult.

Mr. Miller released her and reached his right hand up to massage the chest muscles at the front of his left shoulder. "It hurts like..." A deep sigh escaped him. "Ibuprofen's not going to cut it, but I don't want to be knocked out or all foggy, either. So what are my options?"

She could hardly blame the man. The last time he'd been unconscious, he'd woken up to find his left arm missing. Awareness of her surroundings would be important to her, too, if their roles were reversed. Add to that the nightmare-like state he'd woken up in, and she could understand his reluctance to be medicated.

"Can you describe the pain?" *Shooting, throbbing, burning...* The type of pain said more about its source than most people realized, and Lily was a proponent of treating the cause whenever possible rather than just masking the symptom.

He shook his head. "It hurts too much. I can't think straight. It's hot, though. Can you give me an ice pack?"

Lily moved around to the other side of the bed and rested her gloved hand against the skin visible above his bandages. Heat would be a possible sign of infection and not something to be taken lightly, but no warmth penetrated her vinyl glove. None of the blood cultures had shown infection, either, but still… She yanked her glove off and felt the area again. Good — nothing beyond normal body heat.

"I'm going to give you some hydromorphone for the pain and take your temp to make sure you don't have a fever. Then I'll get some ice for your shoulder. Once the pain's under control, I'll take your BP."

"And you need my temperature to treat my pain because…?" Surliness slipped back into his tone.

"I need to take your temperature before I put the ice on so it doesn't skew the results and hide a fever."

"It's not like you'll be sticking the thermometer in my armpit." A grimace-smile accompanied his words.

Huh. He was joking. Or trying to, at least.

"I'm not much of a rule-breaker, and this is one of those SOP things. Fever could mean infection, which is something we watch for."

Mr. Miller nodded his consent.

Lily's shoulders dropped with relief. The pain clouded his dark eyes more with each passing minute. His stubbornness might well have pushed him to the point where even the hydromorphone wouldn't be enough to bring him back from the edge. She made quick work of administering the medication through his IV and taking his temperature. It was a little high, 99.4 degrees, but not yet alarming.

"I'll be right back." Lily speed-walked her way out of his room and to the small enclave where family members could get coffee, water, and snacks. She cupped a plastic bag under the ice dispenser and hit the button. Once it was full, she sealed the bag off and headed back to Mr. Miller's room. On her way, she snatched a couple of towels off the linen cart. They were scratchy white cotton with a dark blue strip across one end. Somehow that splash of color was supposed to prevent people from wanting to steal them.

"Here we go." Lily folded one towel into fourths and rested it along Mr. Miller's upper chest and shoulder, making sure his neck was protected as well. Then she used the other to wrap the plastic bag before resting it on the edge of his shoulder. She grabbed a pillow from the foot of the bed and tucked it in between the bed's railing and his stump to help keep the ice pack in place.

Her patient closed his eyes and sighed. "How is the ice going to do me any good through all that padding?"

Lily rested the back of her hand against his brow. She already had his temperature. Sometimes, though, people needed human contact. A hand on the forehead was an innocuous enough way to let him know someone cared. "I can't risk getting your bandages wet. Just give it a minute. The cold will penetrate and reach you soon enough. Of course, if you lie here and think about how you can't feel it, it'll only take longer."

She applied hand sanitizer and tugged fresh gloves from the box hanging on the wall. Then she moved to the mobile computer workstation in his room and pulled up the record of his vitals. She entered her reading from a few minutes prior and took note of the trend. His temperature historically ran a bit above normal, ranging from 98.9 to 99.8. A memo in his chart said to alert the resident if it topped a hundred.

The blood pressure machine beeped, and she peered up to get the numbers so she could enter them, as well. A little elevated, but not as high as it would have been before the hydromorphone.

By the time Lily removed the cuff, Mr. Miller's face was relaxed.

"How are you feeling now?"

"Better, and the ice is starting to work, too."

"It's always easier to get ahead of the pain than to catch up to it. The doctor customarily prescribes a regimen of medication so you don't end up in such extreme pain."

He glared. "I wouldn't let him."

That wasn't news to Lily, but at least he admitted it. "It's harder on your body if we wait until you're in agony to treat you. It would be better for you — and for your recovery — if we prevent the pain from reaching those unbearable levels."

His eyes were clearer than they'd been all day, but he didn't hold eye contact for long before looking away. "I don't know about that. People in my family... They don't do well with drugs."

"Do they have allergies?"

He shook his head. "Addictions."

That explained a lot. Mr. Miller was a stubborn man who didn't seem to fear much. Losing an arm didn't bother him nearly as much as the thought that he might become addicted to pain meds.

"We have some alternatives. Are you willing to talk to a doctor so we can try to come up with a pain management plan you're comfortable with?"

He nodded grudgingly. It might not go anywhere, but at least he was willing to participate in a dialogue about pain management. It was a start.

Lily marched to the locker room and grabbed her phone. Then she headed to the break room and tugged her lunch bag out from behind all the others shoved into the refrigerator. She sat down at the small round table and took a deep breath.

Thank You, Father, for the day and for Mr. Miller's progress. Please continue to be with him and his wife as they move forward. And please keep Caleb safe in his job. Amen.

Okay, so it wasn't exactly a traditional meal blessing, but it would do.

Lily took her chicken salad sandwich out and reached for her phone. No texts, but a voicemail waited for her. She took a bite then dialed in to check her messages.

This is Caleb. I'm here with Ashton Raynott…

She fought the gag reflex but couldn't stop herself from spitting the sandwich bite into a napkin. Good riddance.

At the sound of Ashton Raynott's voice, chills shot through her, raising gooseflesh as they went. She closed her eyes and battled against the tears that wanted to spill over. She was safe. Caleb had seen to that. There was no need to react that way.

Maybe she'd been more traumatized that night in the parking garage than she admitted to herself. Lily pressed the phone closer to her ear and played the message a second time, determined to listen to the words this time and not let panic best her.

I'm sorry about scaring you.. I didn't mean no harm… I didn't know what else to do.

She tossed her sandwich in the garbage can. Lily wouldn't be eating it that day. In its place, she withdrew a piece of string cheese and peeled apart its wrapper. She needed to get something into her stomach or she wouldn't be much use during the afternoon and evening hours, and despite any message left on her phone, her patients deserved her best.

Why had Caleb done that? Couldn't he have found another way? What he'd done was invasive. She'd been minding her own business and checking voicemail, then *bam*. There it was.

Should she text him and say what she thought of that message?

No. Better to calm down. He'd warned her in advance who the message was from. She could have hung up or skipped the rest.

Another bite of string cheese.

The message wasn't ugly or anything. Ashton Raynott sounded truly repentant for frightening her. Still…

She finished the cheese and plucked an apple from the interior of her lunch bag. As the swarm of locusts in her stomach settled into a semi-quiet buzz, Lily ate the last of her apple.

Once she calmed down enough to consider herself rational, she collected her phone from where she'd dropped it on the table and tapped at the keys. *Received ur message. Would like 2 have word w/ u.*

His reply was immediate. *I work tonight, but let me bring u dinner. Will u be home by 8?*

Lily stared at the screen. Talking face to face might be best. *Make it 8:30 in case I get stuck in traffic or stay late.*

See you then. Any food preference?

Surprise me.

Lily was still in her scrubs when the knock sounded at her door. A quick look through the peep hole told her who stood on the other side.

When she swung the door wide, Caleb held out a white bag that announced itself with the enticing aroma of chili, garlic, and lemongrass. Staying mad at him wouldn't be easy. He'd brought her food and looked good in his uniform while doing so.

She took the bag and inhaled. "Thai?"

He tipped his hat to her, and even if it wasn't his off-duty cowboy hat, she still found it endearing.

"A little of everything." Next, he handed her a bakery box.

"Cupcakes?"

He shrugged. "I wasn't sure which flavor you liked, so I told them to pack their four most popular."

She set the items on her kitchen counter before turning back to Caleb, hands fisted on her hips. "Either you're the nicest guy ever, or you're trying to make up for something."

"I figured roses would be a bit obvious." He closed the door behind him and relaxed against it. "I'm attempting to find out who in your unit leaked the information about Miller's nurses. Letting him talk to you was my way of getting Raynott on my side."

"Did he tell you where he got my name?"

A frown marred Caleb's face. "Not yet."

Lily crossed her arms. "Why did it have to be on my phone? You could have dialed your own number and let him believe it was me."

Every step filled with purpose, he traversed the room and rested his hands on her shoulders. "Sure, but I'd have been obliged to lie, and that doesn't sit well with me. Sometimes for work I'm forced to be creative with the truth, but this wasn't something I had to lie about, so I didn't."

Goodness, his eyes had grown dark. They'd slid from slate to dark-as-pitch, and as Lily gazed up into them, she wasn't sure she would ever be able to turn away. She licked her lips and tried to concentrate on her words. "I… it surprised me."

Caleb's thumbs rubbed circles on her shoulders. "I'm sorry. I'm sure it was a shock, hearing his voice like that. If I thought for a minute he would do anything other than apologize, I would never have allowed it."

He was a trickster. That was all there was to it. She'd been determined to give him a piece of her mind. That is, until she'd looked in his eyes.

Lily shook her head and shifted her position, turning her back to him. She busied herself taking food out of the bag. "Are you staying, or do you have to get back out on patrol?"

Silence met her question, so she peeked over her shoulder. He stood right where she'd left him, but he waited until her eyes connected with his before answering. "My temporary partner is waiting down in the car, so I should go. Will you still be at the barbecue on Thursday?"

She nodded.

"Are you still mad?"

She was tempted to say yes, but she would be lying. With a frustrated sigh, Lily said, "No, but I wish I was."

Caleb threw his head back and laughed. He stepped closer to her and turned her to face him fully. With a finger under her chin, he gently lifted her face. Humor still danced in his eyes, but so did a lot of other emotions she wasn't ready to identify. He started to lean in, and she fought the urge to meet him. He blinked and pulled himself back the tiniest bit. "You're something else, Lily Ziminski. I look forward to Thursday."

He was gone from her apartment before she could do anything to stop him. Not that she wanted to stop him. Of course not. It wasn't as if she'd needed to force her feet to stay flat on the ground so she wouldn't reach up on tiptoes and lean into the kiss she'd thought was coming. Kissing had been the last thing on her mind. After all, she'd barely met the man, for pity's sake!

Not true. They were well past the *informally introduced* phase. Even so, the two halves of her brain continued to argue the point.

She certainly didn't know him well enough for kissing. Let alone drowning in his eyes or melting under his touch.

Mechanically, she slogged over and flipped the deadbolt on her door. Then she rested her back against it just as Caleb had done. She stared across her living room to her dinner and dessert. There was no denying it. Lily had never reacted so strongly to a man's presence before. She was in big trouble.

Ah, but trouble had never felt so good.

Fourteen

As far as Caleb was concerned, Thursday had taken way too long in coming. A flip of the wrist revealed it was three in the afternoon. One hour until Lily arrived.

He stopped in the kitchen to see if Ma needed anything.

"Shoo! Get out of here! This is what I do best, so let me do it."

He raised his hands in surrender and backed out onto the deck. Only a fool fought with a woman while she was preparing the meal, and he was no fool.

All told, his mom had invited twenty people. They wouldn't all be able to make it, but the truth was, she'd only asked the other folks because he'd insisted she not get carried away and turn it into a two-person party. Even though he would have liked that.

The memory of their almost-kiss had infiltrated his dreams more than he cared to admit. A private party — arranged by his mom, no less — wouldn't win him any points. Not this early in the relationship. She'd made her feelings clear on that front. Ambushes didn't sit well with her. He needed to rein Ma in until he and Lily got a chance to know each other better. Until he could actually use the word *relationship*. Out loud.

He needed to rein himself in, too.

The day before, Caleb had followed Ma's instructions to a tee. The backyard was filled with tables and chairs set up in scattered groupings. The grill was scrubbed and polished, and the insect-repelling candles liberally decorated all the available surfaces.

Another glance at his watch. Three fifteen. Would the clock not go any faster?

With his long stride, Caleb made it to the back of the yard in record time. Once he pushed through the trees standing sentry, he caught sight of his target. He stood on the bank of the burbling creek and listened to nature's melody. Serenity normally washed over him whenever he stood near the water. That spot was his favorite place on his parents' expansive property — now his mom's property. Tranquility, however, remained elusive that day. Caleb sensed its edge nearby, teasing him with its comfort, so he did the only other practical thing that came to mind. He prayed.

God, my heart's racing, my palms are sweaty, and I'm tempted to look in the mirror to check for zits. Please calm me. I'm not sure if it's because I've waited for such a long time for marriage, or because Lily's the one You have for me. Is she the one? Please make Your way clear and help me to treat her the way she deserves. If You could give me a hand, too, so it's not obvious to her how nervous I am, I'd be much obliged. Okay. I'm going now. But so You know, either way — whether she's the one or not — thank You for bringing her into my life. She's something else.

A sensible man would accept that he should take things slow. He would spend time getting acquainted with the woman who'd snagged his interest. He had spent a lifetime trusting his gut, though, trusting the instinct coming from deep down in his soul — the Holy Spirit, by Ma's way of thinking. Did that mean the Holy Spirit was telling him Lily would be a whole lot more in his life than just a woman he'd almost ticketed, just his mom's nurse, or *just* anything?

Any inkling of doubt he held on the matter fled the moment her car pulled into the wide circular drive in front of the house. The sight of that unforgettable silver sedan chased all his nerves away. With a calm and confident stride, he sauntered out to meet her. He was past the point of turning back. She was his, and that was all there was to it.

He decided against telling her yet, though. Sounding like a crazed fanatic wouldn't help his cause.

Caleb tugged his hat down to block the sun as Lily climbed from her car. Her blond hair was free from restraint for the first time since he'd met her. It hung to the middle of her back, mostly straight with a little bounce. She wore makeup, but only a light touch.

Why mess with perfection?

He planned to notice her dress, too. Later. Right now her lips captivated him. A little gloss went a long way toward kissable.

"Glad you could come."

A smile lit Lily's face before she stretched her arm back into the interior and withdrew her sunglasses. She settled them into place. "Thank you. Your mom has a beautiful property."

"You haven't seen anything yet. Come on around to the back. That's where it gets interesting."

She walked beside him. He desired nothing more than to reach out and rest his arm across her shoulders and pull her close to his side. Slow and easy, though. That was how the turtle won the race. Wasn't that how the story went? "Hope you like barbecue."

"I didn't grow up Southern, so it was never a staple in my diet."

"Then you grew up deprived."

Lily glanced around at the front of the house. "Mine's not the only car here. I'm kind of glad. I got a feeling your mom wanted to set us up."

"Would that be so bad?"

A blush painted her face before he took another breath. He took time to admire her dress then. It was pink. Filmy, too. It had sleeves. Sort of. They looked a bit like straps. Strappy things with extra material hanging down over her shoulders. The V in front was modest. The one in back — a quick glance — was deeper. The dress wasn't form-fitting, but it somehow managed to hug her body and flow around her at the same time as she moved. And it matched the color of her cheeks at that exact moment.

"I'm not sure how to take that, Trooper Graham."

They'd rounded the house but hadn't yet made it to the back, where they could be seen by the other guests. The tall hedge that surrounded the property aided the smattering of decades-old trees in giving them privacy.

Caleb stopped walking and tugged Lily's hand so she came to a standstill, too. Compulsion took over — the need to discover if she felt the electricity arcing between them every time they got within reach of each other. "I didn't leave that note on your windshield because I wanted to know how you were. I left it because I needed to know. I haven't been able to stop thinking about you since… well, since I pulled you over, but I'd like to try to pretend that never happened."

Lily stood in silence.

Blast those sunglasses. Caleb reached out and plucked them off her nose so he could get a glimpse of her eyes. Their color put the Texas bluebonnet to shame, but they brimmed with indecision.

"I'm going to kiss you now. You have about three seconds to tell me to stop."

One one-thousand, two one-thou...

Caleb brushed the back of Lily's neck with his right hand as he took a step closer and leaned down. The second his lips touched hers, he was lost. Every Fourth of July he'd ever been to in his life exploded inside his head. His world filled with bright flashes, booming concussions, and the fragrance of summer. He had no idea how long the kiss lasted before he broke away. Every part of his being had been immersed in the sight, sound, smell, and taste of Lily Ziminksi, and one thing was clear — there would be no return to sanity for him.

She didn't throw her arms around him, but on the bright side, she didn't wipe her mouth off or glare at him.

"Are you going to say anything?"

Silence met his question.

If she didn't want that to happen again, she needed to speak up, because if he got his way, it would be happening a lot.

Lily held out a hand, and Caleb realized he still clutched her sunglasses. He returned them to her, and she put them back into place. He couldn't admire her eyes behind those glasses, let alone read them.

"You're not going to say anything, are you?"

She tucked her hand into the crook of his arm. As they began moving again toward the backyard, Lily finally said, "I'm not sure what to say."

"You didn't slap me. I take that as consent to a repeat performance."

She flashed him a sideways smile. "I, uh, got caught up in the moment. Which is dangerous. Maybe it's a good idea if you don't do that again."

That was all the encouragement Caleb needed. She hadn't told him to stop beforehand, nor had she slapped him after. It appeared she'd lost herself during the kiss, too.

He owed Ma a *thanks* for throwing the barbecue together.

Shortly after Caleb introduced Lily to a few of the folks in his backyard, Ma called him up to the deck to help with the meal. He left Lily visiting with an older couple and Julian, their adult son. Julian had some sort of neurological disorder. He was a good guy, but even though he was in his forties, he processed information and interacted with others on the level of a grade schooler.

Much as Caleb had suspected, he, Lily, and Julian were the only people at the gathering whose heads weren't topped in white or silver. He grinned at Ma's scheming as he wondered whether or not Lily realized the age discrepancy.

Ma started handing him dishes to carry out to the deck, and he tried to fit an important conversation in between each item he collected from her.

"So, what did you tell all these people to get them here on such short notice?"

"Didn't I raise you to be honest?"

Dread caused Caleb's heart to stutter before bouncing back to its normal rhythm. "What did you tell them?"

"I told them I'd met the mother of my grandchildren and wasn't getting any younger, so I needed to hurry things along for you two."

"You didn't."

Her silence shouted at him.

"Please tell me you didn't."

"Okay, fine. I didn't."

Caleb, instead of carrying the large bowl of potato salad out to the deck table, ran a hand over his face. "Ma, be serious. What did you tell them?"

His mom, a good foot shorter than him, ambled up and gave him a light tap on the cheek with the palm of her hand. "You like her, right?"

"You know I do."

"Then what does it matter what I told anybody?"

He closed his eyes and tried to count to ten. *One, two, three…* "What did you tell them?"

"I told them my son missed Texas barbecue and that if they knew what was good for them, they'd find time to come enjoy the treat of a lifetime. Well, except for Gertrude and Bernice. They know I've met the mother of my grandchildren."

A Texas-sized sigh of relief slipped through Caleb's lips. Gertrude and Bernice he could handle. They might be gossipy old women, but they were his mom's best friends. Without them prodding her, he wasn't sure Ma would have left the house at all during the first couple months after his dad's death. Those two ladies were priceless gold as far as he was concerned. Caleb loved them because they loved his mom. Not that he planned to tell them so. If he did, they'd start giving him dating advice, too.

Another quick glance into the backyard showed Lily playing croquet with Julian. He'd thought it a silly idea when Ma had instructed him to set the game up on part of the lawn. Croquet had always seemed boring to him. Now, though… now it was the most fascinating game he'd ever witnessed.

A few minutes later, all the food weighed down the back table. His mom tugged the cord on the big cowbell he'd given her a few years ago for

Christmas, and everyone slowly got up from their chairs out on the lawn and shuffled toward the deck.

"Caleb, dear, would you bless the meal?"

He stood behind his mom and rested his hands on her shoulders as he prayed. "Thank you, Father, for the food You've provided and the beautiful day…"

IFTEEN

Lily did her best to concentrate on the words as Caleb prayed but was instead mesmerized by the rumble of his voice. Rather than bow her head and close her eyes, she stared. He fascinated her in a way that both excited and terrified her. And then there was that beard.

She'd never been one for beards. Although she wasn't quite sure his facial hair could be labeled such. His cheeks bore a three-day scruff. Longer than if he'd skipped a day of shaving but not full, either. There was only one word to describe it. Sexy.

The man had a sexy beard surrounding sexy lips right beneath a sexy nose offset by sexy eyes.

Yep. Trouble.

Lily had never been kissed by a man with facial hair before. Not that she made a habit of kissing a lot of men. Of the few there'd been, though, none had sported whiskers of any kind. Neither had they made her forget herself so completely. She'd tried to hide it from Caleb. Her left brain had argued against revealing how rubbery her knees had become or how that one single kiss had robbed her of the ability to breathe.

He was dangerous.

The chorus of *amens* broke through Lily's reverie. She glanced around at the crowd. They were closing the prayer, right? It was just her overactive imagination than put the crowd's *amen* in tandem with her thoughts about Caleb...

Before long, Julian piled food on his plate under his mom's supervision. Hungry as she was, it didn't seem right to rush ahead of all the silver-haired people, so Lily hung back.

"He's a handsome one, that Caleb."

Lily dared a peek and found two women watching her. She felt like a field mouse on a concrete slab under an owl's tree. Any attempt at fleeing would be futile, so she returned the predators' gaze instead. One was shorter than her own five-foot-two-inch frame, and the other was almost as tall as Caleb himself.

"Hi, I'm Bernice, and this is my friend Gertrude." Gertrude the Giant. Hm. Not her kindest mnemonic, but it would do for now.

"Pleased to meet you. Are you friends of Mrs. Graham?"

"Oh, yes, the best of friends. We couldn't come visit her when she was in the ICU because Gertrude here had a cold, and I have a phobia about hospitals and germs. I can go as far as the waiting room, but you won't get me into a hospital room unless I'm dead or unconscious."

They wouldn't be putting her in a room if she were dead, but Lily decided against voicing the thought.

Bernice chuckled and looped her arm through Lily's. "Did you know Caleb has worked in law enforcement his entire adult life? It takes a special kind of man to be that loyal. No matter what the job has thrown at him, he's stuck with it. He's not the sort of man who gives up when something gets difficult."

"All right…" Where were they going with this?

"Gertrude here just mentioned what a fine quality loyalty is in a husband. A woman could do worse than a man who doesn't give up and quit whenever life becomes hard, a man who will fight till his dying breath to keep the woman he loves and do right by her."

Wow. Bernice would put Grandma Louise to shame.

They approached the steps to the deck when Bernice picked up the mostly one-sided exchange again. "Gertrude went on and on about how sexy a man in uniform is."

Gertrude had awfully strong opinions for someone who never uttered a word.

Bernice continued the conversation without stopping for breath. "I'm sure women throw themselves at Caleb all the time. If a woman sets her cap for him, she better snatch him up quick before somebody else cuts in line, if you know what I mean."

Lily was on the brink of telling the women they ought to hurry up and ask him out if they were so interested. Fortunately, before she opened her mouth, the man in question put his hand on her arm and drew her out of the dwindling line.

"Come with me. I want to show you something."

Caleb hustled her inside the house and through the kitchen to a spacious room with high ceilings. A piano rested against one wall while another was filled with books. A pair of well-worn leather recliners held court in front of matching windows, the small table between them sporting an equally aged Bible.

Then Caleb stood there, tugging at the collar of his shirt and staring up as though looking for inspiration among the rafter beams.

"You brought me in here to show me your favorite book?"

"Uh, what did those women say to you?"

Lily laughed. "There's nothing for me to see, is there?"

He shook his head. "Bernice and Gertrude were talking to you, and, well, they can be a little…" His Adam's apple bobbed as he swallowed.

She wondered what else he'd say if she remained quiet but decided not to toy with him like that. The whole situation was too funny. "Bernice kept telling me what Gertrude thought, but Gertrude never spoke."

Caleb nodded. "I've never heard her talk, either, but my mom says she's a regular chatterbox. Go figure." He ran a hand through his hair. "Do I even want to know what they said to you?"

"According to Gertrude, you're perfect marriage material. She thinks you're loyal and hardworking. Oh, and she finds men in uniform sexy. You might want to watch out for her. I think she has designs on you."

"They're my mom's friends." He winced. "They mean well, but..."

Lily waved his explanation away. "Don't worry about it. I have family, too. But I'm telling you, be on guard where Gertrude's concerned. I'm pretty sure she's waiting for an opportunity to lock lips with you."

As soon as the words came out, she regretted them. Her mind was once again filled with thoughts of the kiss they'd shared not too long ago. The way Caleb stared at her mouth, it was a pretty good bet his mind had gone to the exact same place.

"I, uh..." She should go back outside. She should escape before it was too late, not throw herself into his arms and show him how much she'd enjoyed their earlier kiss. Lightning continued to sizzle its way through all her nerve endings.

Caleb took two strides and stood right in front of her. "I'm not sure I can wait three seconds for you to decide." His mouth descended on hers.

A torrent of flame roared through her veins. She should step away. They were alone, and alone was proving a dangerous place for them to be. Lily didn't pull back, though. Instead, she leaned into him and reached up with her hands. His corded muscles bunched as she laid her fingers against his chest then slid them up to circle his neck.

A guttural sound from deep in his throat filled her senses seconds before the squeaky swish of the back patio door penetrated the fog. "Caleb? Lily? Are you in here? You should grab your plates. Otherwise, the ribs…" Mrs. Graham walked into the room and found the two with at least five paces separating them.

If Mrs. Graham's face was any indication, she wasn't fooled by the distance or the way Lily and Caleb avoided looking at each other.

"…Uh, sorry to interrupt. You, uh… You ought to get your ribs before they turn cold. Take your time, though!" She backed out of the living room, waving her hands in front of her. "No hurry. Ribs can always reheat!"

The patio door opened and closed again.

"We need to stop doing that." Lily didn't recognize her own voice. Stop? That was the last thing she wanted, which was exactly why they needed to.

Caleb bowed his head, swallowed, and stared at his cowboy boots. "That might be easier said than done."

She couldn't agree more. "Let's go grab our plates."

He swallowed again. His lips parted as though he intended to speak, but then he closed his mouth. It was too late, though. Her eyes had found their focus.

She blamed him. Those tempting lips of his were far too appealing.

Lily glanced from Caleb to the arch leading out of the living room. Every cell in her body screamed for her to step closer to him and touch him again, but the voice that whispered from deep in her soul would not be drowned out.

She didn't want to leave him, but knowing it was the wiser choice, she stepped toward the arch. "I'll see you outside?"

He gave her a nod.

"We should talk about this." She forced her fluttering hands to her sides. "Not in private, though. I think maybe we should talk when we're not alone."

Another two steps toward the arch.

"Lily?"

She glanced back. In an attempt not to focus on his lips, she made herself look at his eyes. Big mistake. His grey eyes burned with intensity.

"Am I even half as dangerous to you as you are to me?"

How to answer? "I'd like to walk over there and give you a hug because you seem like you need one, and I could use one, too. If I get any closer to you, though, time might stop. The next thing I know, the party will be over, the guests will be gone, and I'll have missed it all because I was in your arms. When I'm near you, nothing else seems to matter."

Not the prettiest speech.

She wasn't done yet, either. "I've always been a slow-moving person. This thing between us kind of freaks me out. I might panic at some point and try to backpedal my way straight out of..." Her hand fluttered in the space between them. "...this."

The tension visibly seeped out of Caleb's shoulders. He was now as relaxed as a cat taking an afternoon nap. "I'm a patient man." A slow smile shaped his mouth, and he was by her side in a couple of his normal long strides.

With a light touch, he kissed the top of her head. "Let's go get some grub. You'll love the ribs."

After they'd eaten their meal and mingled a bit more with some of the seniors — artfully avoiding Bernice and chatty Gertrude — Caleb directed Lily toward the back of his mom's property. They approached the trees, and she hesitated. "I thought we decided not to be alone."

He laced his fingers through hers. "I have it under control. No kissing, I promise."

Lily laughed, and he arched an eyebrow.

"The problem," she told him with a shake of her finger, "is that I might want you to kiss me. What then?"

He glanced skyward, a rueful look on his face. "You sure do know how to make it hard on a guy, don't you?"

They broke through the trees, and she gasped in surprise. "This is beautiful."

Caleb stood, feet planted firmly apart, hands crossed over his chest, his face stamped with one hundred percent pure unmitigated male pride. "This is the corner of Virginia I've claimed as my own. You look good in it."

Pleasure curled its way through Lily's middle. A quick glance around told her a couple of tree stumps were arranged for sitting, so she tucked her dress around her legs and settled onto one. Caleb surveyed the remaining ones before choosing his seat more than ten feet away from her. She smiled. He took his no-kissing promise seriously.

"I'm old-fashioned." He offered no apology. "When God makes something clear to me, I go for it.

No hemming and hawing, no hesitating. Just an all-out leap of faith in the direction He's given me."

Anticipation built inside Lily until her fingers and toes tingled with it. He was going somewhere with this, and while tempted to rush him along, she decided to stay silent and savor every moment of their time in the trees.

"The hooking up and hanging out thing isn't really my way. I'm more of a let's-date or be-my-girlfriend guy. What do you say?"

Not many people would describe Lily as shy, but looking at Caleb sitting there in his jeans, boots, button-up shirt, and cowboy hat, she couldn't help but hesitate. *You've been saying it to me since the first moment I saw concern in his eyes about his mom's condition, Lord. I know in my heart You're telling me yes, but a part of me is scared. This is going fast.*

"I want to say yes, but can we talk about a couple things first?"

"Of course." He nodded his agreement, but his slate grey eyes hid his thoughts.

Lily chose her words carefully. "Different people have different expectations when it comes to dating. We share chemistry, maybe too much of it." How to say it? She'd never been this tempted with a man before, so this was new territory for her. Calling it awkward was like calling a military cargo plane a crop-duster. "I, uh, I wonder what your expectations are for, uh, for..."

Caleb's eyes rounded and his skin flushed hot red — whether from embarrassment or desire, Lily couldn't tell. He parted his lips as though to say something, then swallowed instead. He at last found his voice, and it brooked no room for argument. "I was raised in the Bible belt by God-fearing parents who drummed right and wrong into my head from the time I was old enough to breathe." He winked at her. "So, basically forever. Some things in this world are sacred to marriage, and I don't aim to mess with God's plan for that."

Lily's thoughts jumbled together in her mind until she couldn't sort them out. She should be relieved. She was, too, but… "Good." Her mouth was dry, and she couldn't think of any of the other dozen things she'd wanted to ask him.

Thankfully, he took the conversational baton and carried it. "Sometimes when…"

The deafening sound of far too many sirens roaring past his mom's house drowned out his words. Caleb transformed into law enforcement mode. The casual cowboy disappeared. Intelligence and curiosity snapped in his eyes. He tugged on her hand and hurried her through the trees and back toward the house. The luncheon party had broken up somewhat. Most of the guests had left. Those who remained were gathered on the side of the house, peering in the direction of the wailing sirens.

Sixteen

Caleb made sure his mom and her friends were all safe, then he brushed his lips against Lily's cheek and ran toward the tangle of police cars, fire trucks, and an ambulance three doors down on the opposite side of the street. With most of the homes sitting on more than an acre of property, it wasn't a quick sprint.

As he approached the melee, Caleb flashed his badge to an officer. "I live on this street and heard the commotion. What's going on?"

Behind the officer, firefighters finished unrolling hoses as orders were shouted out. To a civilian it would look like chaos. He understood, though. They were methodical in their approach in everything from how they unrolled the hoses to how they approached the house. No flames were visible from the front, but smoke rose from the back of the property and filled the air with an acrid stench.

The officer looked him up and down before scowling. With the jerk of his arm, he pointed Caleb in the general direction of a weathered man in a suit who stood out of the way of the fire department personnel while giving orders to a young group of officers to secure the scene and silence the sirens.

Caleb was at the detective's side in seconds. He again showed his badge. "I live across the way." With a wave, he indicated his mom's house and the gathering crowd of mature gawkers in the distance. People were coming out of other homes, too, no doubt drawn by the commotion and their own curiosity. "Can I be of help?"

"Graham! What are you doing here?"

He spun toward the voice. His captain stalked toward him, enough fire in her eyes that he could imagine it tripping a smoke detector.

"Captain. I could ask you the same thing." Had he just gotten a break in his case?

"I live here. Why are you on my property?"

Yeah. He really needed to get out and meet the neighbors.

The detective hooked a thumb. "Says he lives a couple houses down."

Captain Browning glanced from the collection of white-haired folks at his mom's house and back to him. "Mr. Graham was your dad?"

Caleb nodded.

The frown didn't leave her face, but she said, "I never made the connection. I knew Mrs. Graham's son had moved in…" Some of the fire left her eyes. "I'm sorry for your loss. Your dad was a kind man and a good neighbor."

"Thank you." He would examine this softer side of his captain later. "Now tell me what happened here."

The captain spit in the dirt. "Arson. Someone set my home on fire."

"Um." No way had the fire investigator been able to determine cause yet.

She fisted her shaking hands at her sides. "Don't you dare patronize me. I was home. I know what I saw and heard."

Never rile an already angry woman. "Any suspects?"

The fire was already out thanks to the efficiency of the firefighters. Property damage appeared to be localized to one outer wall of the garage where the siding was charred and buckled, a small portion even melted. Thankful for the breeze that carried away most of the unnatural chemical smell of burnt vinyl, Caleb studied the burn pattern. Even from this distance and with his untrained eye, he could distinguish the splash pattern of an accelerant. It would be interesting to see what the arson investigator concluded, but for the moment, Caleb was just thankful he hadn't openly questioned her claim of arson.

Captain Browning stared at her house, a myriad of emotions chasing each other across her face. When she turned back to Caleb, her reaction was under lockdown. Her eyes reflected nothing but cold fury. "You and Flannigan. You because proximity gives you opportunity, and Flannigan because he hates me and I'm rattling his cage."

"Flannigan is…?" Being on the list himself wasn't a surprise. The other name was new to him, though, and in her current mood, he didn't dare ask if she had any evidence to back up the claim.

"He'll be running the panel you're testifying before about the maintenance malfeasance out on our stretch of Lee Highway. Virginia's one and only transportation chief."

No matter how Caleb twisted himself around, he couldn't quite reach that itch. There had to be more. "People don't start fires over a couple of random potholes. What else does Flannigan have against you?"

The detective intervened. "You're on the suspect list. That means you're out of the investigation. Head on home."

Amazed he'd been allowed to stay this long, Caleb studied the captain. "I'm not on duty again till Saturday night. Do I report, or am I suspended pending the outcome of this investigation?"

The detective started to answer for her, but Captain Browning cut him off. "I'm the only one who controls which troopers work in my station." She dipped her chin in Caleb's direction. "If they haven't arrested you, I expect you to show up for your next shift." Each word etched into the air with razor blade precision, she added, "Be late, and I'll string you up myself."

He gave her a sharp nod then veered toward home, but a minivan arrived on the scene and three teens tumbled out. The kids, smelling of sunshine and sweat, yelled for their mom as they rushed past. Of all the words he might have used to describe his captain, motherly wasn't one of them. The second she saw the kids, though, her entire posture changed. She opened her arms wide and welcomed them as they all crowded close, hugging her and, Caleb suspected, making sure she was okay.

"She's a good mom."

Caleb peered at the man who had also exited the van. Captain's husband? Brother? Hmm.

"You're Mr. Graham's boy, aren't you? There's a resemblance."

"Yeah. I'm also a suspect in the fire, just so you know."

The man held out his hand. "Roger Flannigan. Pleased to meet you."

He stared from the hand to the man's face. This wasn't a villain with hate dripping from his pores.

Flannigan continued, either ignoring or not noticing Caleb's perusal. "I pulled the kids out of soccer practice as soon as Margaret texted me about the fire, but I wasn't supposed to bring them home till it was under control." He nodded toward the side

189

of the garage. "Looks like it could have been a lot worse."

Home? Nothing added up.

Captain Browning hurried over. "Roger, this is Caleb Graham. He works out of my station."

Flannigan's eyes widened. "Ah. You're going to be testifying about the potholes." He angled his head back to the captain's house. "Margaret talked about the Graham in her station, but I never connected him to the couple down the road. It's the funny thing about living in this neighborhood. We're far enough apart from each other that it feels like the country, but we all keep our distrusting city ways and don't bother meeting each other."

Had Caleb stepped through the looking glass? Eyeing the captain, he asked, "Flannigan?"

The man in question slapped him on the shoulder. "Ah, I should have mentioned I'm the good one."

Implying there was more than one…

Flannigan continued, "I'll let Margaret explain, but remember, sometimes family is a messy thing." Then he pulled the captain close, gave her a kiss on the temple, and whispered hoarsely, "You took years off my life. Let's not do this again." Before she could respond, he moved off toward the teenagers attempting to talk one of the firemen into letting them into the house. His gait was easy, but his hands shook as he tucked them into his pockets. At least he wasn't as unflappable as he seemed.

The captain cleared her throat. "I dated Ed Flannigan back in college but things didn't work out. Years later, I ended up marrying his brother. Roger… He's a good man. We've been together twenty years, married for seventeen of them, and Ed has hated me for every single one of them. He didn't take kindly to the rejection. He's tried interfering with my career at every opportunity. When I married Roger, though, Ed's anger turned into an all-out vendetta."

"That explains how your husband and the transportation chief have the same last name. What about you, though?" Caleb prodded, even if it was only to see how she'd respond. "You kept your maiden name because…?"

Her scowl would have made a puppy wet itself. "You're right. It's none of your concern, but since you managed to show up in the middle of my family drama, I'll tell you. My career was important to me. It was hard enough moving up through the ranks as a woman. A name change seemed like a bad idea at the time. And I'd hoped keeping my maiden name would politically distance me from Ed. Turns out I needed more than political distance. He and Roger haven't spoken in more than a decade. The last time Roger tried to talk sense into Ed, things got ugly. Right or wrong, I made Roger promise me he'd stay away after that."

Caleb pushed for more. "And you think your brother-in-law started the fire?"

She shook her head. "I don't want to think so. It's over the top, even for him. It's..." Captain Browning turned away from him and stared at her kids and husband. When she spoke again, her voice was tight. "There's no reason to suspect him except that I'm angry this happened, and I want someone to blame. If someone doesn't like me, fine. They should be civilized about it and attack me in the media or go after my job. But don't set a single foot near my family. Whoever did this is going to pay dearly for their mistake."

Caleb tucked his hands into his pockets, glad the captain was acting more like herself. "Are you going to let the fire department handle the investigation?"

"It's out of my hands, but don't think I won't be sitting on top of the arson investigator until he figures it out."

"All right, then."

"I think you're one of the good ones, Graham. If you prove me wrong, you'll spend the rest of your life regretting it. Understood?"

Caleb tipped his hat to her. "I wouldn't have it any other way, Captain."

As he walked back toward his mom's house, Caleb mulled over what he'd learned. The transportation chief wouldn't go after his own sister-in-law in such a public manner… would he? It didn't settle well in his gut that Ma was so close to what could be a dangerous situation. He needed to re-evaluate his opinion of the captain, too. Hard-as-nails no longer seemed to fit, not when he'd witnessed the affection between her and her children and husband.

Hm. A woman who refused a name change for the sake of her career didn't seem like she'd be the doting mother type. His captain was a study in incongruity.

His long legs ate up the pavement, and he was bombarded with questions before he even made it back to Ma's lawn.

"Was there a murder?"

"Was it arson?"

"Was there a suicide?"

"Is it a serial killer?"

Caleb held up his hands to quiet his mom's friends. "I think y'all read too much. There was a small fire, but it's contained now. Nobody was hurt."

"Was it arson?" Bernice wouldn't let that particular question go.

"I don't know much about fires. An arson investigator will be handling things, and he'll be the one to determine the cause."

"Gertrude is wondering why so many police responded if it's such a small fire." Bernice, of course, did the actual asking.

Ma fielded the question. "The wife works in law enforcement. County police, I think. Nice family, though. Good kids."

County police... That explained why Ma never mentioned that his captain lived down the street.

Hoping to cut off any other questions, or at least get out of having to answer them, Caleb grasped Lily's hand and tugged her behind him as he maneuvered around to the back of the house again. "Want to go back to the stream?"

She shook her head, and the breeze caressed her hair in a way that made him want to tangle his fingers in it. "I think the tranquility's broken for today."

"I'm not ready to let you go back home yet. Let's go out. Park, movie, zoo, roller rink — you name it. I'm game."

Lily glanced down at her dress. "I'm not wearing my roller derby gear, sorry."

Caleb pulled on her hand until she closed the distance between them. Then he let it go and wrapped his arms around her in a hug. "What do you say I follow you home, we ditch your car, and we go somewhere? Anywhere. We can chase taco trucks or sunsets. I don't care. I just want to be with you."

His heart, previously thrumming at a steady rate, revved up as Lily reached around his middle and snuggled into his embrace.

He'd had a simple strategy: hold her too close to kiss. *Fool!* The full length of her body pressed into close contact with his was… He kept his hands still and arms relaxed, but every fiber in his being argued against his forced nonchalance.

Lily pulled out of the hug. Caleb peeked at her, hoping he'd been able to mask his reaction enough not to scare her off. The quiet in her eyes told him he'd succeeded.

"Sure. Let me go say bye to your mom, then you can follow me home."

She walked away and he made himself relax against the wall, tilting his head back till it made contact. With his eyes closed, he decided to hum a good old-fashioned hymn. That would do the trick more effectively than a cold shower. Besides, what would he say if his mom asked why his hair was wet? In its current muddled state, though, the only tune he could grab onto was a children's song.

The words ran through his head as he hummed. *Jesus loves me, this I know…*

"We're all set. Let's go!"

His eyes snapped open. The sun was sinking into the horizon, and the blaze fell right behind Lily, turning her hair into a golden halo. Life didn't get any better than that.

Caleb wandered around while she went into her bedroom to change.

Her apartment suited her.

The walls were dotted with frames that showcased family and even some pictures of her with patients. The photos were interspersed with an eclectic display of art, but the place still maintained a relaxed and uncluttered air. The living room opened across a bar into the kitchen, which displayed towels, potholders, and other assorted culinary paraphernalia in bright hues of pink, green, yellow, orange, and blue.

When she came back out, he followed her lithe movements across the open space of her apartment. "So, uh, what's your favorite color?"

She shrugged. "I don't have one."

"No favorite color?"

Lily shook her head. "Why do you ask?"

"Your kitchen has its fair share of variety."

Her eyes lit up. "My living room is my relaxing room. Calm colors, soothing décor. My kitchen is my wild and crazy room. Bright colors make me happy, and I like to bake, so I transformed that room into a rainbow. I love spending time in there."

If her living room was neutral and her kitchen was bright... What color was her bedroom? Caleb shook his head to rid himself of the question.

"I listened to the radio on the drive over. They talked about a meteor shower tonight, but we won't be able to watch it from the city." Her voice was hopeful.

"Ever seen a meteor before?"

"Nary a one."

"Well, then, let's load up, and we'll head west until we get away from the lights. What time does it start?"

Lily held up her phone. "I'll look it up while we drive."

"Sounds like a plan." Caleb rested his hand on the small of her back as they crossed into the hallway outside her apartment. "Find out what direction we need to look. I know a first-rate place for viewing the western sky, but it might take a little more work to find a place that'll let us see the eastern sky."

A couple hours later they both lay on their backs on top of a soft quilt in the bed of Caleb's truck.

"What time's the meteor shower supposed to start?" Truth be told, there could be a starless sky above them and it would still be the perfect end to a fabulous day as far as he was concerned.

"Uh…" Lily flipped through a page on her phone again. "Not till two in the morning."

Laughter rumbled in Caleb's chest. "We have quite a wait ahead of us then. It's only ten."

"I couldn't exactly foresee that you'd be so efficient in finding us a place. Besides, the stars are beautiful just the way they are. I'm not sure I've ever seen the night sky like this before."

How many kids did she want? "So tell me why you decided to become a nurse." Better off sticking to safe topics.

Lily shrugged beside him. "It's what I always dreamed of being. I can't remember a time when I thought of doing anything else. I chose to specialize in intensive care because I like the fast pace and unexpected hurdles. It's hard sometimes. We get some tough cases. I suppose a small part of me is an adrenaline junkie, though, and that's the side that thrives in ICU." She shifted. "What about you? Why law enforcement?"

Caleb took a deep breath and enjoyed Lily's perfume. Carried on a light breeze, it smelled like fresh mountain air. "More or less the same. When I was little, I thought I might join the military, but by the time I was in high school, I knew I wanted to go into some kind of police work. That hasn't changed in all the years since. I majored in criminal justice and criminology in college and minored in forensic science."

"That sounds more like training for the FBI, not a small-town sheriff."

"Deputy. The sheriff was still a few years away from retiring, and he wasn't planning on giving up his job any time soon. It would have taken a scandal of epic proportions to get him voted out of office, and he wasn't the scandal type." Caleb raised a shoulder and dropped it. "Honestly, I wasn't sure where I'd end up when I finished college. I got hired somewhere rural, though, and loved it. Turned out my degree was perfect for the job, too. When you work in small-town law enforcement, you wear a lot of different hats."

She leaned over and tugged lightly on his cowboy hat. "I kind of like this one."

A chuckle rumbled in Caleb's chest. "Good, because it's my favorite."

"So you liked working in a rural department…" She let the words hang between them.

"I was more at peace there than anywhere else I had ever been. My mom'll be the first to tell you, I used to be a little high-strung."

"Huh. I've marveled more than once at how calm you always seem. Do you think about moving back to Texas, or are you going to be satisfied living in Virginia?"

He turned to his side and rested his elbow on the bed of the truck, using his hand to prop up his head. "I think I could learn to call it home with the right incentive."

eventeen

Lily couldn't help the jaw-popping yawn.

Caleb grinned at her. "It's good to know I'm such interesting company."

She shook her head. "As an official early riser, I'm usually in bed by now. I can't believe the meteor shower is still hours away."

He stretched out on his back and gathered her close. "Here you go." Her head settled on his shoulder. "At least you have a pillow now in case you fall asleep."

Awareness hummed through Lily's body. She'd never be able to drift off with Caleb so near...

The loud wail of a siren roared through the air around her. Fire! Heat skittered across the tops of her bare feet. Something was after her, waiting and watching. The siren morphed into her name as though the blaze itself were calling to her.

"Lily, wake up." Caleb shook her shoulder. "Wake up."

She blinked as the man hovering over her came into focus. She couldn't distinguish his features in the darkness, but she didn't think he woke her because of the meteor shower. Wonder and awe were decidedly absent from his voice.

"Hear that?"

Lily didn't have to strain her ears. The racket from her dream was all too real. Only it wasn't a siren. "What is that?"

"A pack of coyotes, getting closer by the sound of it. You need to be in the cab where it's safe."

"Okay." Still sluggish from sleep, she sat up and stared warily into the shifting shadows. "Is it unlocked?"

Before she realized it was coming, Caleb snatched her up and sat her on the side of the truck bed. She grabbed on to keep her balance while he jumped out the back and closed the tailgate. He came around to where she rested on the edge of the bed, and he drew her down into his arms before opening the driver-side door and setting her down behind the steering wheel.

She blinked in the interior's sudden light.

"Scoot over so I can climb in, too." Humor sparkled in his eyes.

Lily scrambled across the middle console and into her own seat, and Caleb climbed in behind her, shutting the door with the solid sound of metal against metal.

"I'm afraid the meteor shower will have to wait for another night. We'll try to catch the next one. I knew they had coyotes out here, but I thought being so close to an urbanized area would force them into smaller packs. The one we heard was anything but small. At least a dozen strong if sound's anything to go by. It's not worth the risk."

The cobwebs began to clear, and Lily glanced at Caleb. "Would you have stayed if you'd been alone?"

He frowned as he started the engine. "Is that important?"

Of course he would have. He was leaving because of her. Should she be angry or flattered?

Lily caught a glimpse of the heat in Caleb's eyes.

Flattered. Definitely flattered. She might not be crazy about someone making decisions for her, but she could get used to the look in those grey orbs when he was set on protecting her.

"I'm sorry I fell asleep. That's not like me."

He offered her a half shrug as he steered the truck onto the road. "Like you said. You're an early bird, and I'm a night owl. It didn't bother me. I liked watching you sleep." Then he winced. "But not in a creepy peeping Tom kind of way."

How could she not find him endearing with sweet talk like that? "Did I snore?"

Caleb reached over and laced the fingers of his right hand through those of her left. "Even if you did, you're still the most beautiful sight I've ever seen."

Polar ice caps would melt at the sound of his voice. How did she stand a chance?

"You keep saying things like that, and a girl might get the wrong idea."

The only light in the truck's cab came from the dashboard. His lips moved in the dim blue glow. "I'm pretty sure you're not getting the wrong idea."

"He's insane! He has to be... Right?"

Lily was nowhere near ready to give up her rant when Lyza cut her off. "Child, you got to admire a man who recognizes what he wants and goes after it."

Together the two women worked to reposition an unconscious patient.

"You don't understand," Lily countered. "I think he's talking about marriage, and we barely know each other."

Lyza leaned back and surveyed their handiwork. "Does that look comfortable to you?"

Lily eyed the patient lying on his side, knees bent, pillows offering support behind him so he wouldn't slump onto his back, his arms propped around another pillow to give them a different position, and the feet and knees protected with pillow cushions as well. "I'm sleepy just looking at him. I need a pile of pillows like this for my bed at home." She threw Lyza an admiring smile. "You always pay so much attention to the patient's comfort, even if they can't tell you what they like."

"Mm-mm-mm," Lyza half-hummed. "If I were ever sick like this, I hope someone would care enough to want me to be comfortable, too. Anyhow, no way is a patient of mine getting bed sores, not on my watch."

Some nurses programmed the bed so that it shifted automatically, alleviating the risk of pressure sores, but Lyza came from the days before automated beds. "Nothing feels as good as curling up on your side after being forced to lie on your back for hours."

Lily gathered up the soiled linens and put them into the proper receptacle. "He's moving so fast. I'm not sure what to do."

"Y'all have chemistry?" Lyza lifted her eyebrows in question.

"More than I know what to do with."

"Never felt this way about another man before?"

"Never, and I'm not some starry-eyed teenager, either."

"You talk it over with The Man Upstairs yet?"

Hiding a cringe, Lily nodded. She'd been taught it was disrespectful to refer to God as The Man Upstairs. That was the other nurse's way, though, and Lyza genuinely meant no disrespect by it. "I've talked, but I'm not hearing a response."

"You got your emotions all twisted up and fit to be tied, don't you?"

They stepped out into the corridor, and Lily threw herself down into a chair at the nearby nurse's station. The chair spun her in a full circle before it came to a stop. "Is it normal for men to move so fast?"

Lyza clucked her tongue and took the other available seat. She brought the patient's chart up on the screen so she could document the position change. "Some men spend their whole life not knowing who they are or what they want. They make lousy husbands because they're never satisfied. They're always wondering if the gal across the street is gonna make them happier. And they blame their woman, their job, or their children whenever they don't feel fulfilled, but the truth is they're unfulfilled because they're clueless about life. That's not a real man."

The older nurse yanked her reading glasses down far on her nose and peered at Lily over the top of them. "When you find a man who knows his own mind and what he wants, and plans to dedicate the rest of his days to making you the happiest woman on earth, girl, you snatch him up. From everything you've told me, this trooper is the type of man that holds on. Not the smothering, wife-beating kind of hold-on, but the rock-in-the-storm kind of hold-on. That's a man who won't leave you high and dry when life gets rough and when bad things go down. A man you want by your side when your child's diagnosed with an incurable disease, when your parents sue each other over the family china, or when you do your monthly check and discover a lump in your breast. No point in having a man stand beside you all the days of your life unless he's strong enough to hold you up whenever you need to lean on him."

Caleb was all those things. If she could choose someone to lean on, she would pick him. "You're sure it's not weird that he's moving so fast?"

"I met my Charlie at a friend's birthday party." Lyza chuckled. "We were datin' by the next day and engaged before two weeks passed."

"How long was your engagement?"

Lyza snorted. "We got a little impatient for the weddin' night, and we weren't even engaged yet. After that, Charlie insisted we wed right away. He wanted to do right by me. Knew each other less than a month when we tied the knot. That was more'n twenty years ago."

"Did you marry him because you slept with him or because he was the one?"

Lyza brushed the question aside. "I ain't condonin' what we did, mind you, but I like to think my body understood what my brain was havin' a hard time accepting. I don't think I'd have ever ended up in bed with the man if I hadn't recognized all the way down to the core of my bein' that I planned to spend the rest of my life with him." Lyza shook a finger at Lily. "Don't think that's stopped me from preaching abstinence to every single one of my babies, though. What I did was wrong and dumb and reckless. I count it a blessing every day that God saw fit to work it out for good."

"You couldn't have known each other very well when you got married. I always thought engagements were supposed to be long so people can become more familiar with one other."

Another snort filled the corridor. "My marriage has been an adventure, one that's never been boring. It hasn't always been easy, and we had some hard adjustments to make early on, but we were committed, and we stuck with it, and I've never regretted it."

"Lily — front desk!"

Her head snapped up. The charge nurse waved her over as she conferred with Arlene Norval, the nursing director. As Lily approached, the director pointed to her. "In my office. Now."

Lily's heart raced as she sat in Arlene's office waiting for the woman to join her. What had she done wrong?

She wiped her sweaty palms on her scrubs, plucked off any stray lint or hair she could find on her clothes, and smoothed the wrinkles developed over the course of the day. The sudden opening of the door caused her to jump. Arlene strode in, took a seat in front of the L-shaped desk resting against the wall in the corner of her office, and faced Lily.

"We have a situation on our hands. Someone under Secret Service protection was shot, and he's in our OR."

Political drama. Not at all what she'd expected.

"Your name is already linked to a high-profile case. Rather than put another nurse in the spotlight, I'd like to ask you to take on the daytime care for this patient. With Mr. Miller gone to rehab, it should be easy enough."

"I'm on today and tomorrow then off again."

She nodded. "With your permission, I'll rearrange the schedule so that you're with him until he's transferred out. I'll be doing the same with his night nurse who, incidentally, also worked with Mr. Miller."

"What about my other patients?"

"Someone from the float pool is taking over their care. They'll be in good hands."

High-profile cases weren't unusual, but they weren't commonplace, either. Lily had seen them handled in different ways over the years. The last nursing director had given no special treatment, dropping those cases into the regular rotation like every other patient in ICU.

She hadn't lasted long in the job.

"That'll be fine," Lily told Arlene. "How long are we talking? I can work four or five days straight with no problem. If it goes much longer than that, though, I'll need a day off."

The director concurred. "I had a brief word with the surgeon. Five days should be enough for recovery. He'd be on the main floor if he weren't a VIP. There's one other thing you should be aware of…"

Lily waited, shuddering inwardly at the tone in the other woman's voice.

"Secret Service is all over this one. They tried to get permission to confine the nurses to campus housing so they could keep you under lock and key. I fought it. You can stay on campus if you want, and they'll guard you. Otherwise, you're free to go home between shifts, but be aware that Secret Service is more uptight than usual. They could change the rules at any time. An Agent Whitehall is heading up the security force that will be present in ICU. I'm sure you'll run into him."

Word came from the OR: surgery was done and had gone well. For security reasons, the recovery room would be bypassed. The patient would be sent straight to ICU. Lily got her first look at him when she went downstairs to take over custody from the OR nurse. Post-op patients didn't often make a memorable first impression, but she wanted to commit this one to memory. Who knew? He could be president someday.

She studied her patient, but true to form, there wasn't much to notice about him just yet. He was covered neck-to-toe in hospital blankets and had medical equipment jumbled around him. There wasn't much to see beside his wheat-colored hair with a little grey at the temples. Oh well. Barring anything unforeseen, she'd have plenty of time to get to know her patient later.

In the meantime, she found herself dealing with three men in suits and sporting firearms. The Secret Service agents wouldn't allow any of the orderlies near and insisted on pushing the bed themselves. The only medical personnel allowed on the elevator besides her was a respiratory technician.

Lily resisted the urge to clear her throat as she contemplated the somber-faced men accompanying her patient. "When the doors open, we'll need to turn left, but you'll swing the bed right first so we can get it situated the way we want. He needs to go down the hallway head first in order for us to make it into his room smoothly."

None of the men said a word, but when the elevator doors parted, the agents did exactly as she'd told them. Within minutes, the patient was settled into his room. The charge nurse came in to help transfer all the monitoring equipment from displaying on the portable screen to the in-room one, and the respiratory technician worked to wrap and secure the corrugated tubing to the respirator so the excess wasn't in anybody's way.

Lily, who had grabbed a couple minutes in the break room with the television before she'd been called down, had a good idea who her patient was. Jefferson David Taylor, the most likely man to snag the Republican nomination for president. He was younger than the other candidates, unmarried, physically fit, reasonably attractive, and he had been shot. The media didn't seem to know anything about the shooting other than the fact that it had occurred. What she'd learned in the few minutes she'd caught of the news program had been pure speculation.

Once Mr. Taylor's stats were displayed on the in-room monitor where she could screen them, Lily angled around and stared at the three Secret Service agents. "You can't all stay in here, and any of you that are going to be on this unit need to go scrub in. You leave the unit, fine. The second you come back in, you scrub again. No exceptions."

One of the agents advanced and held out his hand to shake. He cut an imposing figure with his tall frame and broad shoulders. His angular face sported a scar near his right eyebrow, drawing her attention to green eyes. He wasn't a bad-looking man. He might even have been handsome were it not for the scowl. She didn't take it personally, though. After all, he was Secret Service. A scowl was practically part of the uniform.

Lily, already gloved up, took the offered hand. As soon as he released it, though, she removed her gloves and dropped them in the wastebasket before pulling on new ones. He quirked an eyebrow before looking at the other two agents. "Go on. Do as she says. I'll wait till you're back."

After they left, he returned his attention to her. "I'm Agent Whitehall. I'm responsible for Mr. Taylor's safety while he's here at the hospital."

Had he been in charge earlier in the day when the shooting occurred? Lily pursed her lips. Could he be trusted with her patient's wellbeing? Surely he'd been vetted, but still… "Was it an assassination attempt?"

Not an ounce of emotion showed on the planes of his face. "I'm not able to comment on that at this time."

"Why so much security for a candidate? He doesn't even have his party's nomination yet."

Without rolling his eyes, the agent gave the impression of having done just that. "Secret Service takes over security for all major candidates one hundred and twenty days prior to election. Exceptions to that rule can be made by executive order only."

"We're more than a hundred and twenty days out. So executive order…" Had the president been aware of a threat against Taylor's life? "Was he under your protection at the time of the shooting?"

Agent Whitehall frowned and offered a brief shake of his head. "Your man here is almost a shoo-in for the Republican nomination, and if he gets that, he'll be running against an incumbent president. It would reflect poorly on the current administration — and that president — if every reasonable measure was not taken to secure Mr. Taylor's safety and complete recovery."

Of course. It was political.

Lily shook her head and shoved her curiosity back into its box. "I don't care about his politics, and I don't care about yours. People coming and going from this room are strictly limited for his health. The more people in and out, the more germs he's exposed to, the greater the chance of infection. MRSA is not something you want to play with."

Agent Whitehall gave her a curt nod. "Two agents are stationed outside the ICU entrance, two in the conference room, and one in the hallway outside Mr. Taylor's room. I am the only one who will be allowed into his room. No matter what anybody else tells you, they're not authorized to be in here."

"Family?"

"Mother died years ago. Father is flying in. No wife or children. He has two brothers, but they'll wait to hear from their dad before deciding whether or not to make the trip."

Hopefully the father wasn't the overbearing type. Not that she wasn't used to dealing with all sorts of family members, but Lily didn't relish the thought of a high-maintenance parent in addition to her patient's weapon-carrying shadows. She retrieved the blood pressure cuff from its hook.

Whitehall stared her down, steel in his eyes. "You're to speak to no one about Mr. Taylor. Not even your pet goldfish is to know you are acting as his nurse; is that understood?"

Agent Whitehall was an intimidating specimen, but he was in her domain, and she wasn't cowed. "If you want to stay on the unit, I suggest you go scrub in."

He didn't budge.

"Don't worry. I don't have a goldfish."

The corner of his mouth twitched.

Eighteen

Caleb's phone dragged him from his daytime slumber. He didn't recognize the caller ID and answered with a gruff, "What?"

"Trooper Graham?"

Sitting up in bed and rubbing a hand roughly over his eyes, Caleb tried to make his words civil. "That's me."

"This is Rick Peters down at the impound lot. We had another break-in, this time in broad daylight. Nobody saw anything, and the cameras caught squat."

"How do you know the place was broken into, then?"

"I did like you suggested and requested an around-the-clock K9 presence. They went nuts. When the officer and I got to the scene, we couldn't find anything, but the dogs were all gathered at a spot along the fence line and barking like they'd caught the scent of a juicy steak."

"Huh. This is different than last time, right?" Sleep was gone and Caleb was alert. The cogwheels in his mind picked up speed.

"Yeah. Last time they cut through the fence, wrecked the cars, and made an all-out mess. This time, if not for the dogs, we'd be clueless that someone had been in here."

"Why call me? You think it's related to my car? Maybe they were after something else altogether."

"I've been running this lot for more than a decade. Aside from a couple of petty attempts here and there, these are the only two break-ins I've ever had. That don't say coincidence to me."

"Me, either." Messy job the first time. Too tidy the second time. The break-in was hired out for the first go-round, and the amateurs made a shamble of things. Whoever paid them decided to do it himself the next time and was more careful — or skilled — at the task. The perp hadn't been aware that dogs had been brought in, which at least meant no one at the impound lot was in his pocket.

"All right," Caleb said. "I'm on it."

"Malik, this is Caleb Graham. I was given your name as the tech-in-charge. I'm calling to check progress on a late model maroon car delivered to y'all earlier in the week."

"I was just reviewing the notes." The tech's voice came through the phone. "Are you coming down, or do you want a verbal report?"

"Verbal's fine." He wanted answers; he didn't care how he got them. "Tell me what you know."

"We haven't gotten to it."

Caleb bit back his frustration. Why'd the guy even ask what kind of report he wanted? "You still have it, though, right?"

"Yes, sir. Locked down tight in the garage and still sealed in plastic, but a triple homicide and two vehicular manslaughter cases are ahead of you. It'll be a little while before we make it to your car, but it's secure until then."

"There was a second break-in at the impound lot, and it's likely that's the car they were after. We need to figure out what the thieves want sooner rather than later."

Malik sighed. "You and everybody else. I'm doing the best I can."

Caleb decided the easiest way to accomplish something would be to get the captain on his side. He walked into the station two hours before his shift and approached her office. Captain Browning glanced up and scowled at him. "Come in."

After he closed the door behind him, he settled into one of the uncomfortable chairs across from her. "You know the pothole case, right?"

She nodded.

"The impound lot was broken into and every similar car was forced open. That one happened to be locked in a garage the thieves didn't get to."

Her eyebrow moved upward in that don't-you-dare-waste-my-time way of hers.

"Rick runs the lot, and he went over the car on his own then again with me. We couldn't find anything. I had it transferred to the crime lab so their techs could give it a once-over."

The eyebrow climbed higher. "Overstepping yourself a bit, don't you think?"

"Rick brought in dogs after the first break-in. He got hit again today, but the perp left no evidence and isn't showing up on camera anywhere. The only way he knew was because the dogs went ballistic. This guy wasn't sloppy like the last one."

The eyebrow lowered back to its normal resting place. "Whoever is behind this hired an amateur the first time and either hired a pro for the second go-round or decided to do it himself. Or herself."

Caleb gave a brief nod. "I wondered if you could light a fire under the folks at the crime lab for me."

Captain Browning scowled. "Did the kids you caught in the car admit to anything?"

He shook his head. "Mum's the word. They confessed to the drugs and stealing the car, but if anything else is going on, they're not telling. If the techs at the lab find me some leverage, I might be able to push them."

"Hm." Her eyes pierced him. "Is that in your job description?"

"I'm doing what needs to be done. Why delegate when I'm perfectly capable?" He stood.

"Let me make some calls."

"Thank you, Captain. By the way, has the arson investigator learned anything?"

Her words were a guttural growl. "Amateur arson. It's looking less like a professional job and more like some idiot had too much to drink and exercised extremely bad judgment. Accelerant was cheap tequila you can get at any liquor store. Ignition source is in question, but they're still working the case."

Caleb winced. He wasn't sure which was worse: being the target of a planned attack or the victim of a random crime. As a cop, neither sat well, but the latter chaffed a bit more. "Does that mean I'm no longer on the suspect list?"

"That's outside my jurisdiction." She gave the barest hint of a smile.

He made a move for the door.

"About what I said that day… That is to say, when I named suspects…"

He'd never seen his captain at a loss for words, but he could guess what she was trying to say. "You were angry."

"It wasn't rational to suspect Flannigan. I knew it at the time. I just…" Her voice broke. "What if my kids had been home?" She dropped her gaze and lined up the pens on her desktop. When she looked up again, the old captain — full of unbridled confidence — was back in place. "I'm surprised the folks at the crime lab gave you the time of day."

"I might have bluffed a little."

She still wasn't done with him. "How is Sebastian working out?"

"Ask me in a week."

He shut the door behind him and headed toward the locker room.

"Hey, Graham, what are you doing here so early? Our shift doesn't start for a while yet, I thought."

"I could say the same about you, Sebastian. Why are you here so early in the day?"

"Eager to learn, my man. Eager to learn."

A quick glance at the clock told Caleb his shift was coming up sooner than he'd realized. "I'm going to step out for a bit. I'll be back in time for roll call."

He jogged out to his truck and drove the half mile down the road to a deli he'd found. After he'd ordered, his fingers flew across the keys, pulling up Lily's number as he sat down to wait for his order.

Her voicemail kicked on, and he listened to the musical sound of her voice. "You reached me, but I'm not here. Tell me what you want, and I'll think about calling you back. Now go be a blessing to someone today."

The message evoked a smile he didn't bother to fight. "Hey, Lily, it's Caleb. I thought I'd say hi before I go on-shift. I hope you've had a good day."

When his sandwich arrived, he devoured it then returned to the station, resigned to what was most assuredly going to be a long night with Sebastian riding shotgun.

Caleb's alarm woke him the next afternoon. He rose, ready to tackle the day… and to see Lily. She hadn't called or even texted the night before, and worry gnawed at his gut.

I get that women aren't wired like men, Lord, but I'm not used to insecurity. The chemistry is there, and it's strong. Help her understand we're meant to be. And if I'm wrong about this, then, well… then I don't know. Help me accept it, I guess, because I'm not going to want to.

Caleb climbed down the stairs and greeted his mom. "How's your day been so far?" He tipped his hat to Bernice and Gertrude. "Ladies."

Ma smiled at him. "Just fine, dear. Why in your uniform so early? Are you going to let me feed you before you leave?"

Bernice spoke up. "Gertrude hasn't been able to stop talking about that young lady of yours. So charming and kind. She'd make a wonderful mother, that one."

"I'll be sure to tell her Gertrude thinks so." He'd expected his mom's friends to take up her campaign, but he'd fooled himself into thinking they'd take a more subtle approach. He should have known better.

Bernice wasn't done, though. "Has Gertrude ever told you the story of how she and her husband met?"

He'd never heard Gertrude tell any story, but that wasn't the best time to say so.

"They met at a dance on base one night and married a week later. Quite the whirlwind romance."

"What about you, Bernice? How did you and the late Mr. Pinceer meet?"

"Oh, we were sufficiently boring, I'm afraid." Color filled Bernice's cheeks. "He courted me for several months before my father gave consent. Tradition was important to my folks."

Caleb was willing to bet his breakfast that there was more to the story than his mother's friend admitted to, but he'd let her keep her secrets. For now. He'd tuck it away in his arsenal in case she and the talkative Gertrude ever cornered Lily in conversation gain.

With that pleasant thought, he kissed his mother on the cheek. "I'm leaving early so I can stop by the hospital on my way in."

Her raised eyebrow said it all. The hospital was in the opposite direction from his station. "Visiting someone?"

He tweaked the tip of her nose. "Stay out of it, Ma."

"Me? Interfere? Never!" Her laughter chased him out the front door.

On his way, Caleb pulled into the mall's main parking lot and trailed the line of cars snaking around the white-lined spaces, heading instead into the underground parking garage. It was a popular mall feature. Summer or winter, people liked to avoid the weather.

Once he got through the last bit of security, the guard allowed him through the heavy metal door. "Second door on the right."

Marching down the hall, Caleb was anxious to be done there and on to his next destination — the hospital.

The instant Caleb opened the door to the drab white-walled room, Nick spoke. "You called a meet. What's up?"

Still standing, Caleb tugged a flash drive from his pocket and slid it across the table. "My final report."

"You sure you got everything you need?"

Caleb nodded. "I need to stay on until the transportation hearing. I owe her that."

Nick's head bobbed. "Sure. No problem. How are you liking the undercover work?"

"I'm not. I don't like deceiving people. Straight-up investigation is what I signed on for, not this."

"This situation came up unexpectedly, and your background was too perfect to pass up. Undercover won't be a regular part of what you do for the attorney general. Covert, sure. Clandestine, occasionally. Undercover — not so much."

"It would have been nice to be informed that the woman you had me investigating lived…" Caleb leaned in. "On. My. Street."

Nick threw his hands up. "I thought you'd figure that one out on my own. I can't help it if you're Mr. Antisocial."

"What about the relationship between the transportation chief and Captain Browning? Did you ever plan on telling me that?"

A frown tugged down the corners of Nick's mouth. "It was need-to-know."

"Right." Sarcasm gave the word a polished veneer.

"This isn't about you and me. This is politics."
Caleb grimaced.

"I trust you to be unbiased, but the twenty pairs of eyes that are going to go over these reports with a fine-tooth comb won't. No prior knowledge means an objective report. If anyone has even an inkling of a doubt about it, your report will be considered biased and will end up tossed out with the trash."

"Which is what the chief's going to want, I'm sure."

Nick grinned, and his eyes lit up. "That's my battle."

His friend's animation was contagious. "You've always loved a good fight." The time had arrived to go fishing. "Had Flannigan been blessed with the foresight to realize you would one day be gunning for him, he'd never have taken a single step toward the wrong side of the law."

Nick didn't take the bait. "We good?"

"Yeah. Let me stay with this one at least to the hearings. As soon as I'm free and clear, I'll let you know, and you can officially welcome me to your investigative team and give me some real work. This driving around all night looking for speeders and weavers…"

"Don't knock it. Chasing down one of those weavers got you Lily, didn't it?"

"I'm still working on that one."

Caleb started to turn the doorknob when Nick stopped him. "Catch ne news lately?" Expectation etched its way into Nick's question.

"No. It's called sleep. You should try it sometime."

"There's been a high-profile shooting in the District. The media's on it, but Secret Service and the FBI are silent. No press release yet, but unless I miss my guess, the vic's either going to be at Georgetown or your girl's hospital. I wouldn't be averse to you sharing it with me if you learn anything from her."

The remainder of the drive to the hospital was uneventful. The radio filled him in on the shooting, but details were sketchy at best, and no word on the victim's condition or location was released. The increased security in the lobby, however, answered the *where* question.

When he got to the ICU floor, a glance inside the waiting room told him it was empty; not unusual for the pre-dinner hour, he supposed. He approached the doors to the unit, but two men in suits and with earpieces gave him pause.

"I'm here to speak with one of the nurses. Do I ring through like normal, or do I tell the two of you?"

One man remained stone-faced. The other answered, "Use the intercom."

Caleb pressed the button to reach the reception desk inside the unit.

"Can I help you?" The tinny and disjointed question spoke to the need for an upgrade in the communication system.

"I'm here for Lily Ziminski."

The suited men tensed.

"Uh." The person on the other end of the intercom hesitated. "I can't let you in."

"If she's not busy, can you ask her to come to the door?"

"Sir, I'm afraid we're going to have to ask you to leave." The same man as before spoke, but they both stepped forward.

"Why?" Caleb fisted his hands and stopped shy of demanding they answer. "Is Lily all right?"

"Sir, you need to leave now."

"What's going on here?"

The men next placed their hands on their holstered service weapons, and Caleb tasted the bitterness of defeat. He pivoted with near military precision and marched back down the hall.

He paused in the waiting room and brought Lily's number up on his phone before tapping the *Call* button. Voicemail picked up, which came as no surprise. "Hey, there. I stopped by the hospital, but ICU's under lockdown. Call and tell me you're okay." He ran a hand through his hair before adding, "I'd like to hear your voice."

Caleb was not a man used to being thwarted. Irritation with nowhere to go fueled his steps as he returned to the parking garage. It didn't help that he found a man leaning against his truck. A fed, by the look of him. "Are you lost?"

The man stood to his full impressive height and held out his hand. "Agent Whitehall, Secret Service."

How'd the guy know which vehicle was his, let alone find it with such speed? "Y'all aren't doing a very good job of making friends around here."

The agent dropped his hand and eyed Caleb's uniform. "You state police?"

He ignored the question. "What can I do for you?"

Agent Whitehall crossed his arms and leaned back against the truck. "I'm the agent in charge. Those men turned you away on my orders. I happened to be in the general vicinity of the nurse you wanted to speak to when I gave the order. She didn't appreciate how I handled the situation."

Caleb relaxed and smiled for the first time since arriving at the hospital.

"I was sent to deliver a message."

Caleb restrained his mirth, but it didn't come easy. "The high and mighty Secret Service agent demoted to errand boy?"

"You're pushing it. I can take the message with me and walk away."

"You won't do that." Caleb watched Whitehall for weakness. Either the man didn't have any, or he was good at hiding them. "You do that, and you'll have to tell Lily you didn't deliver it."

A chink showed in the armor. The agent almost smiled. "She's off at seven then driving home, but she has to turn in early. If you can call between eight and nine, she'll be able to talk. Otherwise try again tomorrow night."

Caleb nodded. "Is everything okay on the unit?"

"Your nurse is fine. That's all you need to know."

"The Taylor shooting?"

Whitehall pushed himself away from the truck and began the walk back to the hospital. He tossed his parting words carelessly over his shoulder. "You should leave now or you'll be late to work, Trooper Graham."

The sky was dark, but the road he was on remained bright with street lights. Caleb couldn't get away from Sebastian, but it was time to call Lily, so he pulled over and gave his co-pilot the radar gun.

She came on the line after first ring. "Sorry about earlier."

"No problem. I only have a minute, but I wanted to hear your voice."

"I'll be working the next three or four days straight, maybe longer."

"You're not avoiding me, now, are you, darling?" He meant it as a joke, but Lily's hesitancy made him sit up straighter. "Are you?"

She sighed. "It's been a long day and I'm tired, which can make me blunt."

"I can handle blunt." Sure, he could handle it. But would he want to this time? The tone of her voice made him think not.

"I'm not avoiding you, but part of me is glad for some time apart."

Sebastian started chattering about a car speeding two miles over the limit.

"Someone's with you?"

"The captain has me working with someone, one of her recent hires. Can you at least tell me why?" Caleb was so sure about the desire of his heart, but did he possess enough certainty for both of them?

"I can't think straight when I'm around you."

A smile shaped his mouth. "That's not so bad, is it?"

If she agreed, she wasn't about to tell him so. "I'm used to thinking things through, to being clear-headed. I forget myself with you, though, and that makes me question the wisdom of spending too much time together."

Sebastian's chatter went up an octave as he clocked a car at seventeen over the limit.

Your presence is requested in the town of silence.

That was what his dad used to say.

"I have to run, Lily. You can have your space these next few days, but know one thing. I'm going to spend every waking minute wishing I was with you. Now go get yourself some rest. G'night, sweetheart."

Nineteen

The siren came to life right before Caleb disconnected the call, startling Lily into dropping her phone.

Drat and double drat. Whether he realized it or not, Caleb had made sure he would be all she thought about for the next several days. How had she ended up in such a mess? Not that he was a mess. In fact, he was kind of... perfect. How could anyone be that charming, good-looking, smart, and funny? It shouldn't be legal.

In fact, they needed a new division in the state police, an entire team dedicated to arresting people who have too much sex appeal. With all the distraction they caused, they were a public menace! Of course, there'd be only one person on their Most Wanted list...

Lily retrieved her phone from the floor and set it on her nightstand before crawling under the covers. Tomorrow would be on her doorstep in a blink.

The way her luck had been going, she would probably spend every minute between now and her morning alarm dreaming about Caleb, too. Triple drat!

Agent Whitehall, shadows under his eyes, sat in a chair in Mr. Taylor's room. Lily ambled in and greeted him with a bright, "Good morning!"

He scowled.

"You were here all night. You can't be very effective if you don't sleep."

The scowl deepened. "He had a restless night. Somebody needed to stay here with him."

She could point out that his night nurse had been in to check on him every fifteen minutes, but given the growl in his voice, she decided against it. "I thought his dad arrived."

"He's taken a room at the south end of the hospital campus. He went back there a couple hours ago." Agent Whitehall stretched and cracked his knuckles. "You should see him this afternoon."

Lily checked Mr. Taylor's vital signs and recorded the numbers. "He used to be a senator, but he resigned to run for president, right?"

The Secret Service agent inclined his head.

"Once a person is no longer a senator, do you still refer to him by title? Should I call him Senator Taylor or Mr. Taylor?"

The scowl eased a shade. "He prefers mister."

Lily pulled on the Velcro to release the automated blood pressure cuff. "Mr. Taylor, I'm going to move this to your other arm so we can give this one a break." As she snugged the cuff into place, she looked at Agent Whitehall. "I understand his blood pressure was up and down quite a bit during the night."

Whitehall nodded. "The doctors don't have a clue why."

"I'm just talking here, so you can tell me to mind my own business if you want, but it seems like you know Mr. Taylor pretty well. I'd heard he didn't get Secret Service protection until after the shooting."

Before Agent Whitehall could answer, Lily glanced up at the monitor while reaching for her patient's wrist. There was a fluctuation in his heart rate.

"Is something wrong?"

She spared the agent a quick look. "Nothing that I can tell. He might be waking up, though. Was he conscious at all during the night?" Lily had already been briefed by the night nurse. The question was a habit more than anything else. Loved ones needed to feel like a part of the medical care, too, and whatever the relationship between Agent Whitehall and Mr. Taylor, it was more than the met-yesterday-for-the-first-time variety.

The doctors, making rounds, had been three doors down at her last check. They'd be arriving soon enough. No need to go chasing them.

"Mr. Taylor, can you hear me?"

The agent jumped up from his seat and drew close to the bed. "Taylor! Taylor, you in there? It's Whitehall. I got your twenty. No worries here, but man, you have got to wake up."

The fingers on the patient's right hand moved, and Agent Whitehall grabbed them in what looked to be a bone-crunching grip. "I'm right here. You're safe."

"How's our patient doing today?" Dr. Jordan stood in the doorway.

"He's working on waking up."

Dr. Jordan triggered the wall-mounted can of hand sanitizing foam as he strode into the room and slid the door closed behind him. After rubbing a liberal amount of the sanitizer into his hands, he plucked two vinyl gloves out of the box marked *large* and tugged them onto his still-moist hands.

Lily moved out of the way as the intensivist approached the bed. "Mr. Taylor, can you hear me? My name is Dr. Jordan. Blink if you can hear me."

They all watched the patient's eyes. No movement. Her attention was split between patient and monitor.

"Stimuli?" The doctor's demanding voice grated on her nerves.

Did Whitehall's turn-bones-to-dust grip on the patient's hand count? "No, sir. He started showing signs of waking, and you were already on your way, so I thought it best to wait."

Dr. Jordan barely acknowledged her. "If there's no change, give him a bath in thirty minutes to prod him along."

Lily grunted her agreement as the doctor left the room.

Dr. Jordan no sooner stepped over the threshold than Agent Whitehall muttered, "I liked last night's doctor better."

She bit back her first thought. How to be diplomatic? "Personality and skills don't always match up. Mr. Taylor is in excellent hands, I can assure you." It was true. Dr. Jordan was an exceptional doctor, even if his bedside manner tended to be off-putting.

A sudden spike on the monitor caught Lily's eye. She frowned at Whitehall. "Is it possible your friend here could be awake but choosing not to let us know?"

The agent shrugged.

Most patients instinctively panicked when they woke to an ET tube in their throat. That was what she'd been waiting for, but no panic was forthcoming. Yet the increased heart rate would indicate… "Has Mr. Taylor ever been badly wounded before?"

Whitehall gave her a stone-faced look. "Why?"

"His heart rate says he's awake, but his response says he's not. Most people wouldn't be able to pull that off unless they were used to medical equipment and knew what to expect."

Lily, whose eyes had been on the monitor, glanced down and found Mr. Taylor watching her. She smiled at him. "Hi, there. Were you hiding from the doctor?"

The slightest nod was her answer.

She patted his hand. "He needs to be informed so we can see about getting your ET tube out, okay?"

Another nod.

The doctors had only moved down two doors as they continued with rounds. Lily poked her head out the door and signaled one of the residents. "He's awake. Can you tell Dr. Jordan?"

That was never going to be quite good enough, though. The resident came into the room, said a few words to Mr. Taylor, listened to his heart with a stethoscope, and checked his capillary refill rate before going on her way to inform Dr. Jordan.

"What was that all about?" Whitehall's disgruntled question was aimed at Lily.

"We're a teaching hospital." The man's stare made her want to apologize. "The intensivist is sort of like the professor, and the residents are the students. They all want to impress him."

In the following hours, Mr. Taylor was relieved of his ET tube and catheter and allowed to walk around the room a bit. At the moment, he was off his feet and sitting up in bed awaiting his lunch of soft foods and liquids.

"Mm-mm. I hope they have lime gelatin for me."

Lily raised an eyebrow. "You actually like that stuff?"

"When I was in the service, it seemed like that was the only kind they ever served in the mess hall. It started out as something I dreaded seeing and, wouldn't you know it, it ended up as a comfort food."

The tray arrived, filled with broth, cooked wheat cereal, juice, and orange gelatin.

"Too bad." The patient's words came with a relaxed, down-to-earth ease. Not political polish like Lily expected.

He lifted his spoon and stirred the still-steaming cereal. "Whitehall, you need to catch some shuteye."

"I'm on the job."

"Agents are stationed in the hall and at the entry to the ICU. I'm pretty sure I'm safe here. I need you at your best for when they transfer me out of here. Get some sleep."

Whitehall glared but got up and strode over to the dry erase board. After writing a phone number on it, he wheeled on Lily. "This is my cell. You call if anything comes up. Anything at all."

She nodded, and he slipped out the door.

Mr. Taylor nodded toward the vacant doorway. "A guy couldn't ask for a more loyal friend."

Lily examined her patient, but professionalism prevented her from asking the prying question on her mind. "He stayed up with you all night, kept your dad company. I wasn't here, but I heard about it."

"We go way back. The kind of friends that stick together even when one of you gets political."

Lily didn't say anything, and he took a bite of his cereal. "Most people have questions for me."

"I know everything I need to. Unless your pain level has changed. Has it?"

Mr. Taylor shook his head. "Either you're uninterested in politics, or you're voting for someone else."

Lily nudged his tray a little closer. "Don't neglect the most important meal of the day." Once he continued eating, she decided to humor him and answer his unspoken question. "Strange as it might be around these parts, I don't eat, sleep, and breathe politics. I follow enough to know who I want to vote for, but I don't obsess over it."

He started to laugh, then winced and put a hand to his side where they'd removed the bullet. "Someday, when I do marry, it'll be to someone who couldn't care less about politics. I don't suppose you're available?" An overdone wink accompanied his words.

Lily shook her head. "Finish your lunch like a good boy, and I'll find you at least a dozen eligible nurses interested in taking you up on that offer."

"Let me guess. All over the age of sixty or younger than twenty-five?"

"Something like that." She grinned at him. "Now, eat. I'll be at the desk right outside your door doing some paperwork. You can call for me or press the button if you need anything." Lily pointed to the wired controller that she'd placed within his reach.

"Yes, ma'am." He offered her a two-fingered salute.

The day moved on without incident. The senior Mr. Taylor and Agent Whitehall came to an understanding. The patient's dad would spend the nights in the hospital room while the other slept, and during the day they would reverse.

Lily's shift finished on time that night. "Mr. Taylor appears to be on the mend," she told the night nurse. "He's in good spirits and has a healthy appetite." No need to mention his affinity for green gelatin.

As Lily left the hospital, her phone rang. "Hello?"

"Hey, darling, how was your day?" Caleb's voice was warm as molasses syrup.

"It was ordinary, enjoyable even. How about yours?"

His words were a low rumble, still heavy with sleep. "My day's just getting started. How long until I can see you?"

"At least a couple more days. I'm not sure exactly."

He sighed. "That sounds like forever."

A little pressure felt good, but too much and the weight became crushing. Caleb was on the sizzling side of that fine line, but she needed to get off the phone before he crossed over. "I'm about to enter the parking garage. I'll lose the signal once I go in."

"Oh." His disappointment slow-danced its way across the connection.

She should go find a baby bear to kick while she was at it.

"I guess I should let you go. I'll call tomorrow."

Lily stopped walking and stood outside the garage's entrance. "Don't take it personally. I'm tired. I should be better company after some sleep."

Why couldn't she make up her mind? She was drawn to him on every level, especially when he was within reach. Yet she had bursts of ambivalence that didn't make sense, even to her.

An epiphany came to her as she passed the guard booth. "Aha!"

The uniformed man inside the small windowed structure eyed her suspiciously.

Caleb had their future all planned out. Even if she wanted the same things as he did, she didn't want him choosing them for her. Like when they'd fled the coyotes. He'd decided what they should do without asking her, and a part of her had resented that. Then she'd peered into his eyes and understood that everything he'd done had been to protect her, not to run roughshod over her, and she'd been okay again.

When she was away from him, like the last few days, she balked at the way he seemed to have decided where they were going, the route they'd travel, and how long it would take to arrive. If Caleb was right in front of her, though, and she could peer into his eyes, she'd want the future she saw there as much as he wanted it. Maybe more. So which part of her brain made the most sense? Should she listen to the doubts that creeped up when they were apart? Or her certainty when they were together?

"How are you this morning, Mr. Taylor?" Lily smiled at her patient as she circled her fingers around his wrist to check his pulse.

"Much better. I wish they'd let me out of here."

"The doctors are being cautious, and despite feeling better, your wound is serious and you underwent a lengthy surgery. Staying with us a bit longer won't do you any harm."

"That's what I keep telling him." Whitehall spoke from a shadowy corner.

Lily nodded to him then rounded and gave her attention back to Mr. Taylor. "Your breakfast tray should be here any minute. The night nurse told me you were bright-eyed and bushy-tailed at four o'clock this morning."

"I'm an early riser." The patient plucked at lint on the hospital blanket. "And it's noisy in here."

Lily laughed. "You have that right. The only people who rest well in ICU are the ones who are too ill to realize what a madhouse it is or too tired to care."

Mr. Taylor tilted his head to the side, quizzical. "There was a lot of yelling last night. What was that about?"

The previous night's goings-on had been discussed during the morning meeting. It was a tragic situation. "A family got some bad news and emotions ran high."

Sadness tugged at the corners of his mouth, and true empathy shone in his eyes. "Life isn't always easy."

She resisted the urge to pat him on the hand. "No, it's not, and sometimes people are put into unimaginable situations and forced to make impossible choices."

Whitehall spoke up. "Do people often react with anger when they receive bad news?"

Lily's eyes flitted to the Secret Service agent. "Everybody handles stress differently. Some people shine like cut crystal, others like rusty garbage pails. It's not our place to judge."

"Someone getting irate and carrying on like last night — that must make it harder on all of you." Mr. Taylor scrutinized Lily far too closely for someone who'd been shot not long ago.

She slanted her head to the side, considering his words. "Both are hard, but not for the same reasons." It was true. Her heart ached when she worked with those families who were the epitome of kindness despite whatever tragedy they faced. When dealing with a belligerent family member, though, her heart tumbled and somersaulted inside her chest. Both hurt, but in different ways.

A knock interrupted them. "Breakfast!"

Lily stepped over to the door and accepted the tray with a "Thank you," effectively blocking the deliverer's line of sight into the room. Then she angled back around to Mr. Taylor. "You're off the liquid diet. We'll see how you do with some real food today. It smells good."

Once the patient was settled in with his meal, Lily left him alone and went out to the desk. He didn't need constant care, but since she wasn't permitted to take on any other patients as long as he was in ICU, she was often at loose ends. She contemplated starting a game of solitaire when Agent Whitehall trailed her out of the room.

"Hospitals are boring."

Lily smirked. "You don't have to stay here, you know. I'm sure there are other assignments. You could always ask for a transfer."

"Nah. We go way back. My family owes him. I learned about the order coming down from the White House and asked for the assignment."

Squinting, she searched the agent's face. "You talk to him like you were in the military together, but you're too young, aren't you? You could have served under him, but not with him."

Agent Whitehall nodded in the direction of the hospital room. "He served with my older brother. Saved his life. Like I said, my family owes him. No matter what his politics are, he'll always have my vote. He's as solid as they come."

She wasn't overly familiar with his platform, but Taylor's campaign to capture the Republican nomination for president was no secret. "More of a liberal, are you?"

His nod was crisp and to-the-point, much like the man. "Born and raised, but that doesn't guarantee my vote. I won't choose politics over character. Taylor might be a conservative, but he's got integrity. I trust him to say what he means and mean what he says. That's worth something in my book."

Silence settled between them. Lily was done with the chart, and Mr. Taylor, finished with breakfast, was asleep. She didn't want to disturb him, especially when she had no medical reason to be in his room. Under strict orders to keep watch at all times, though, she couldn't wander far.

"So what was all the ruckus last night? I wasn't here, but Taylor's dad mentioned it, too."

Lily gave him her best glare. "I can't discuss that."

The corner of Whitehall's mouth tilted up. "I'm pretty sure my clearance is higher than yours."

"Clearance has nothing to do with confidentiality, and you know it."

Hoping to end the conversation, Lily returned her attention to the computer screen. He stopped prodding, so it must have worked. She couldn't discuss the details, but she'd heard about the episode along with everyone else during the morning briefing. A woman had been declared brain dead. Her husband and the father of their three children had understandably not taken the news well. He'd just been a bit more vocal — and physical — than most. Given that security had been called in, Whitehall had to know the details of the incident. The Secret Service agents posted in the unit would have been fully aware.

"You patch things up with your boyfriend?"

Lily's eyes shot to the agent. "You presume too much."

He chuckled. "Touchy, huh? Why? He seems decent enough."

She frowned as she tried to sort it out for herself. "We only met a couple weeks ago, and he's talking happily-ever-after. Is that weird?"

Whitehall shook his head. "He been married before?"

Lily answered with a return headshake.

"Had any serious relationships? Live-in girlfriend?"

She shook her head again. "He says he's been waiting for God to bring the right woman into his life."

"Sounds like he's decided you're that woman." It was a statement, not a question.

"You seem to understand better than I do." Lily narrowed her eyes. "Why is he in such a hurry to move the relationship forward?"

Whitehall leaned back in his chair. "I can't tell you what's going on inside your man's head, but I'll let you in on a little secret about men in general."

"Give. I'm sure I'll find your insight fascinating." She propped one elbow on the desk and cupped her chin in her hand.

"Your man's not in a hurry to involve himself with just any woman. If he had a string of divorces behind him, it would be different. That's not the case here. He's obviously waited this long to get married for a reason. Now that he's found the woman he believes is right for him, marriage is going to be the only thing on his mind. Your trooper's smart enough to know what he's got with you and man enough to want to get you locked down before you come to your senses. That's the way men think."

Lily sat back in her chair again and fidgeted with the hem of her scrub top. "Doesn't he worry that we're going too fast? That we might not be well-suited?"

Whitehall shook his head. "Men don't think that way. We don't wait around twiddling our thumbs while we try to decide whether our feelings are real or not. Once a man knows how he feels about a woman, he acts on it. Plain and simple."

Lily raised an eyebrow. "Are you sure? It seems to me that most people these days have long engagements."

"Trust me, it's at the woman's insistence. Men would get it over with if given the choice. They'd put that little gold band on her finger and their name on her Social Security card as soon as she accepts the proposal."

She rolled her eyes. "You make all men sound barbaric."

"Now you're getting it. And if you find one you can love despite that, then you grab ahold and hang on, because the next one won't be any better. Barbary is written into our DNA."

Lily wasn't ready to buy off on the agent's explanation of men and relationships, but he'd given her something to think about. Even though she was tempted to protest and say all men couldn't be like that, a part of her thrilled at the notion that Caleb wanted to make such a public claim to her.

The senior Mr. Taylor was settled into his son's room, and the night nurse had been briefed on the uneventful day. The younger Mr. Taylor had politely demanded newspapers. He was currently devouring every article written about the shooting while Fox News played on the television. His campaign advisor wasn't allowed on the unit, but the two had shared several phone calls throughout the day.

As Lily collected her belongings, an uncomfortable tingle made its way down her spine.

When she glanced up, Agent Whitehall was there, his right shoulder leaning against a locker a few down from hers. "I'm escorting you home tonight."

Her heart rate kicked into high gear as she took in his somber expression. "Why?"

"Word leaked that it was an assassination attempt. We tried to keep that part under wraps and let the public think it was a random shooting. It was a long shot, and it blew up today. Hospital security is dealing with a media frenzy in the lobby. They had better step it up, or every nurse leaving work is going to be questioned by reporters. I'm taking you out a back way, driving you home, staying the night, and bringing you back in the morning."

"You're staying the night?" Did she grumble about the media, an assassination attempt, or the fact that her car would be left in the hospital garage? Of course not. She went straight for the spending-the-night part of the conversation.

"I'll be on the couch, another agent will be in the lobby, and county police have increased patrols in your area."

It was much worse than with Mr. Miller. Media had circled the hospital then, but he had only been a local hero. Reporters had been keenly interested, but they hadn't descended like a starving wake of vultures eager to rip apart the exposed flesh of the vulnerable. Mr. Taylor, on the other hand, was a national figure. Millions of Americans felt personally invested in him and clamored to know about his well-being, and the media would give no quarter.

Lily sighed with resignation. "Very well."

She trudged after Agent Whitehall through various doors and corridors until they got to the cafeteria's kitchen. He led her out through a service door to a waiting car.

TWENTY

Caleb sat in his truck and waited for Lily to arrive home from work. It was his night off, and he needed to see her. Things had been unsettled between them the last couple times they'd talked, and it gnawed at him. Her whole *needing space* thing had come out of the blue. He wouldn't rest well until they resolved their differences, even if he didn't entirely understand what those differences were.

He growled in frustration as he tapped out a steady beat on the steering wheel while keeping his eyes glued to the front of Lily's building.

What if she parks on the other side and goes in the back?

Caleb was about to dial her phone when a dark sedan drove by on its way around the building. Lily rode in the passenger seat.

What in the world…?

Faster than a Texas wildfire spreads, he was out of his truck and entering the apartment's lobby. He arrived at the elevators in time to meet Lily and the Secret Service agent who'd earlier leaned against his truck in the hospital parking garage.

He could tell the minute she caught sight of him. Her eyes widened and her cheeks filled with color. Guilt? Or something else?

The agent, though, only nodded. "Join us for the ride up?"

Once the elevator doors closed behind them, she took a step closer to Caleb. "There's a problem with the media, and Agent Whitehall thought it prudent to escort me home."

The agent's eyes sparkled. "I'm spending the night, too. You know, to keep her safe."

Lily scowled at the agent. "On the couch. With another agent in the lobby."

Caleb took a deep breath and let it out. His eyes never leaving Whitehall's face, he said, "I'll spend the night. I have my off-duty weapon and will be able to give her a ride to work in the morning."

She paled. "I'm not sure that's such a good idea."

The agent's face remained somber, but his eyes continued to laugh. "Yeah... I don't think that's our best play here."

Caleb stepped closer to the agent. No way was he letting Whitehall spend the night at Lily's.

The woman in question elbowed her way between the two men and placed her hand on Caleb's chest. "What has gotten into you? This is not a competition."

The elevator dinged and the doors slid open. Dots danced in front of his eyes as cameras started flashing. "What the...?"

Whitehall pushed the button, closing the doors and taking them up to a different floor. Then he spoke into his communicator. "Media on her floor. Get them out now."

They got off the elevator three levels up from Lily's apartment. It wouldn't take long for the vultures to catch up with them. As they exited, though, Caleb reached back in and tapped the button for the top floor — and every one in between. That would buy them some time, but they still needed to find a place to conceal themselves. Overeager reporters could climb the stairs as easily as use an elevator.

Whitehall waved them down the hallway. With not much more than a couple of clicks, the door to a furnace room was unlocked. "It'll be tight, but let's ride it out in here. My men will remove the reporters."

Lily entered first, Caleb right behind her. Whitehall came in last and relocked the door. "Make sure your phones are off. We don't want a call from Grandma giving away our location."

No sooner did the words settle over them than feet ran past their hiding spot. Lily shifted behind Caleb, reaching for her phone most likely. He extracted his from its case on his belt and thumbed it off.

The moment the echo of feet passed, Caleb took a micro-step toward Whitehall — all their confined space would allow. His mouth next to the man's ear, he murmured, "I'll stay the night. You keep everyone away from her building."

She moved again. A pointy jab to his kidneys told him she'd crossed her arms. They were in a furnace room, so she couldn't be cold. That left angry or scared. He hoped for the former. Anger he could handle. Fear... Thinking of Lily being afraid made him want to sink his fist into something — or someone.

"How do they know where I live? For that matter, how did they find out I'm his nurse?" A fly walking on water would have sounded like a train whistle compared to the volume of her words.

She didn't say who her patient was, but Caleb knew. He twisted around in the tight space. It wasn't in his nature to turn his back to the threat, but right now Lily was more important.

She hugged her shoulder bag close to her body, arms crossed over it. Even in the darkness, the tension in her posture was visible. He hauled her lightly into a hug. "It's all about..."

"Money." The men's responses were in perfect unison. A team of synchronized swimmers couldn't have done better.

Caleb rubbed her back. "Someone figured out a way to capitalize and sold the information. It's the American way."

"Who would do that?" Lily sought answers, despite the fact that they sometimes couldn't be found.

They fell silent as more feet ran down the hall.

Once the feet passed, Caleb answered. "It could be another nurse. A janitor. Even the person who brings the meal tray."

She shook her head. "How would they find my address, though?"

Whitehall interjected, throwing the answer over his shoulder. "All a reporter needs is a name. If they're good at their job, they can figure the rest out. None of that matters, though. You need to stay focused. You're no good to anyone if you're hysterical."

Caleb grinned at Whitehall's *faux pas*.

"Hysterical?" Lily's voice rose an octave. "You think I'm hysterical?"

The agent sighed. "That came out wrong."

Whitehall must have received a message over his communicator then, because a second later, he unlocked the door and stepped out into the hall. "Come on, the floor's been cleared."

Caleb gave Lily a quick squeeze before moving away from her and into the hallway. Turning to Whitehall, he asked, "That fast?"

The agent nodded. "Neighbors had already complained. The police were only a minute or two behind us pulling into the parking lot. My man in the lobby explained the situation, and they got it cleared. They're rounding up stragglers on the other floors, but the stairwell's secure so we can go down to her apartment unseen."

The men made a move toward the stairs, Lily buffered between them.

Once they were safely in her apartment, Caleb crossed his arms and faced the Secret Service agent. He had an uncanny urge to flex. "I can look after her tonight. You just keep the reporters away from the building."

Whitehall removed a couple business cards from his wallet and handed one to each of them. "Call my cell if anything comes up. We're stepping up security now that they've targeted Lily."

Caleb didn't like the sound of that. *Targeted.*

Whitehall bent in close to Lily's ear and whispered something.

Then he stopped in front of Caleb, and his words held a quiet threat. "There is more to you than you want people to know, Trooper Graham. I will see you forcibly removed if your secrets endanger her in any way."

"Does stir fry sound all right?" Fatigue resonated in Lily's words.

"Go relax. I can cook dinner." She'd changed out of her scrubs and insisted she was fine, but exhaustion weighed her shoulders down more than a fifty-pound sack of flour.

Her brow wrinkled, whether with suspicion or disbelief he couldn't tell. "Are you sure?"

"Of course. Sit down, put your feet up, or do whatever you normally do at the end of a long day."

Lily frowned at him. "I normally cook."

Caleb shooed her out of the kitchen before he started digging through her refrigerator and looking for something to throw together. He was an intelligent single man who'd cooked for himself for years before moving back in with his mother. Somehow it didn't sound quite as impressive when he added that last part.

Thirty minutes later, he found Lily fast asleep on the couch, the grey television remote loosely cradled in her hand. He squatted down beside her and put his hand on her shoulder. "Dinner's ready, sleepyhead. Come on over to the table."

She stirred but didn't wake.

Unable to resist, Caleb leaned in and kissed her forehead, her cheek, and the side of her neck that was exposed to him.

Lily started to stretch, and he angled back to admire the sight of her sleepy movements when the remote fell from her loose grasp. It bounced off his shoe and somehow managed to crash into the bottom of her glass-topped coffee table.

She jolted awake and sat up, almost bumping her head on his chin. "What was that?"

He stood and offered her a hand up. "The remote. I was trying to wake you for dinner, and you dropped it."

"Hm. I was having the strangest dream." Lily bypassed the dining table, went to the kitchen sink, and washed her hands.

A nurse on the clock and off. The thought brought a smile to his face.

Once she sat at the table, they bowed their heads, and Caleb prayed. "Thank you, Lord, that Lily made it home safely. Please be with Jefferson Taylor and the agents protecting him. Keep the media away from the hospital personnel. Be with everyone in that ICU tonight, Lord. So many people are hurting in one way or another. Use the staff, the volunteers, and the visitors to lift the spirits of those in need and remind people of Your love. Amen."

"Amen."

Lily took a couple bites before smiling. "This is delicious. You liked the sound of stir fry?"

He assented. "You mentioned it, so I figured you had everything. I sliced some vegetables, cut up some chicken, and voila!"

He finished his meal first. "Are you okay with me spending the night? I'll sleep on the couch."

She set her fork down and gazed droopy-lidded across the table at him. "I'm too drained to care. If I weren't so tired, I might say something about how I'd rather be asked than told, though."

She broke eye contact and picked up her fork again. The loss of her gaze might just have saved his sanity. A man could drown in those eyes. Some men — like him — might even want to.

"Point taken. Would you prefer Agent Whitehall's presence?"

She swallowed before answering. "I'd prefer not to need anybody here at all."

He rearranged his silverware for the umpteenth time as she finished off the last of her zucchini. "I was waiting for you tonight so we could talk."

Her shoulders slumped. "Can it wait for a couple days? Until this whole thing blows over?"

Before Caleb could answer, Lily swung her hand through the air between them, aiming at nothing and everything. "Never mind. I want to say something, and you need to listen."

He nodded.

"I'm fine with spontaneity and last-minute decisions when we're talking about what's for dinner, but when it comes to big life stuff, I move at a more deliberate pace. You're the complete opposite, and it's exhilarating and electrifying, but it's also terrifying."

Caleb started to say something, but she cut him off with another hand-slash. "You don't live your life in slow motion. I get that. When you decided to move from Texas to Virginia, you made the decision one day and moved the next, right?"

He waited. Any answer he gave would only serve to add miles of height to the molehill she was turning into a mountain.

"Well? Did you?"

"I had to give my notice at work, so it was more like two weeks."

"But you gave your notice the day after you decided?"

Heat climbed his neck, and he couldn't even say why he was embarrassed. "The day of, actually."

A look of triumph passed over her face. Then she started chewing on her bottom lip as she frowned. The triumph told Caleb she had a competitive streak. The frown told him she still didn't know what to do with him.

He sat back in his chair and folded his hands behind his head. "Different isn't the same as bad."

"You're right. Different doesn't have to be bad. We also seem to be alike in some ways. I'd say we're both used to taking charge, but that doesn't always work in relationships, does it? There has to be give and take, and I'm not talking about orders."

Lily stopped for a breath, and Caleb probed for more. "Do you want me to back off?"

She paled. "I need enough space to hear what God's telling me. That's all. I can't hear Him when you're close."

"Because I'm so different?"

"Because my equilibrium gets wonky when you're around! My emotions become so loud they drown out God. Being around you feels good, but I'm afraid if I make decisions based on what I'm feeling, I'll end up making bad ones. I need to know I'm making the choice God wants for me."

"So we slow down and I give you space. No talk about weddings or what it would be like to be married or how many children we'll have."

"No more kissing, either," she interjected. "Definitely none of that."

Caleb stood and walked around the table, holding out a hand to help Lily up. "Come on. You need to go to bed." He escorted her to her bedroom door. Her toes were crossing over the threshold when she spun back, raised on her tiptoes, and kissed him on his scruffy cheek.

"I thought you said none of that."

She shrugged. "I can't be held accountable for anything I say when I'm tired. I talk a lot of nonsense."

Her bedroom door closed, and he scratched his chin.

Huh.

Women were confusing.

Caleb, who had slept all day, didn't bother with a blanket or pillow for the couch. He palmed the remote and flipped through channels until he found a college game. Then he turned the volume up a couple of clicks before stepping over into the kitchen. He was as far away from Lily's room as he could get in her apartment when he pulled out his phone and dialed.

"Hello." The voice on the other end was thick with sleep.

"It's Graham. Did you catch the news tonight?"

Raynott squeaked. "Uh, maybe."

Right or wrong, the charges against the man had been dropped. The DA had decided not to prosecute. Caleb just hoped Ashton Raynott still felt guilty about scaring Lily.

"Her face is plastered all over every television screen in the DC metro area because somebody leaked important and private information about an ICU nurse. I need to find and plug the leak. If you want to right the wrong you did before, tell me about your source so I can keep her and any of the other nurses involved safe."

Caleb listened to a mumbled and long-winded explanation.

As soon as he got off the phone with Raynott, he called Whitehall. He wasn't sure yet whether or not he liked the agent, but his gut said he should trust him. And his gut tended to be right.

"Hello." Not a trace of sleep in this voice. "What do you need, Graham? Want me to come spell you? I wouldn't mind spending the night with Lily…"

"I know how word about the nurses got out."

"Oh?" Whitehall's phone demeanor went from lazy to crisp in a single syllable.

"Lily was accosted in the parking garage not too long ago."

"I'm familiar with the situation."

"Assuming the reporters got her name the same way he did, look for a woman in her fifties who delivers linens to ICU."

"How did your guy find her?"

Caleb recited what he'd been told. "He knew someone who knew someone who knew about a lady who worked at the hospital and had money trouble. Raynott's willing to give an official statement if needed. He can detail it all out for you."

"Do you have a name?"

"It's like Lucy but longer — he couldn't remember. Lucinda, Luciana, something like that. Linens. Intensive care. That much he was certain of. She should be pretty easy to pinpoint."

"Did your guy tell you why?"

People sometimes did wrong things for right reasons. The noble reasons didn't make the actions any less awful, though. "A family member was put in prison. She ended up with three small children. Finances got tight. Paperwork got lost somewhere along the way, and she's not getting any state help. That's the story she fed him, anyway. It needs to be checked out."

Whitehall whistled. "Trying guilt now, huh? I send her to prison, and the kids get indoctrinated into the system. Their family gets broken, and it becomes my fault instead of the woman's who broke the law."

Caleb glanced toward Lily's door. She was a soft touch. Something like this would matter to her. "Just check out what she said before you act. Find out if she's a decent person who screwed up or if she's…"

"Yeah. But if she leaked information about someone under Secret Service protection… She messed with the wrong agency this time, and the consequences will bear that out. I'll do some digging into her situation first, but I'm not making promises."

"Keep me apprised?"

"Sure. Now go get some sleep. Or eat some popcorn. Do something besides yakking my ear off all night."

Caleb disconnected the call and removed his hat long enough to run a hand through his hair. If he wasn't careful, Whitehall would be buying them BFF bracelets to wear.

A fifty-year-old black and white movie was keeping Caleb company when Lily's alarm shook the entire apartment the next morning. He glanced outside. The sun was still a long way from making an appearance. No wonder she needed such a loud alarm. It couldn't be easy to force yourself out of bed that early on a daily basis.

When she came out of her bedroom, he greeted her with a cup of hot coffee and an egg and bagel sandwich. "I wasn't sure what you liked in the morning, but I figured this would be good for you."

She took it with a smile. "Agent Whitehall is waiting in the lobby. He'll drive me back to the hospital."

Caleb's chest burned with an emotion he'd not experienced until recently. Jealousy. "I can take you."

Lily shook her head. "He has to sneak me in through some secret passage. It's all very clandestine."

With a curt nod, he angled away from her to look out the window.

"Come on," she murmured. "I want to talk to you on the way down."

Caleb snatched up his keys from where he'd set them the evening before and followed her out the door, tension in the clenched muscles of his jaw.

They strolled toward the elevator, and Lily looped her hand through his arm. "I'm more alert this morning, and I think I can do a better job of explaining myself. Are you willing to listen?"

"I'm always interested in what you have to say." Caleb pushed his tension away and took a deep breath.

She grinned. "There's that Graham charm again." The elevator doors slid closed behind them. "I've been an independent person a long time. You have a strong personality, and you're used to getting your own way. I think a part of me is afraid of being swallowed up by that. I want the same things you want here, but I find myself rebelling and pushing back rather than walking alongside you."

"You figured all that out while you slept?"

She gave his arm a semi-hug. "Sometimes sleep is the only time I'm still enough to listen to God."

"So this is about you finding a way to be yourself, no matter who I am or what I do."

A crisp nod was her answer.

"Good. I happen to like you the way you are, and I wouldn't want you to change anything simply because I somehow convinced you that you had no choice. I can be pushy. Ma says I bully people for their own good. There might be some truth in that." He tugged her arm free of his, laced his fingers with hers, and brought her hand to his mouth for a kiss. "If this is going to last, then you need to be able to go toe-to-toe with me and still come out okay."

A smile curved the delicate corner of her mouth. "What would we go toe-to-toe over?"

"The color of curtains, of course." He winked at her.

Caleb had no more than bid Lily and Agent Whitehall farewell when his phone rang. He recognized the number. "What can I do for you, Captain?"

"You can get your tail down here right now. I've ordered all the kids back in."

"Did the lab find something?"

He could imagine the impatience on her face as she huffed over the line. "No. I'm doing this to waste everybody's time."

"Can you at least tell me what they found?" Caleb climbed into his truck and buckled in.

"Gunpowder in the trunk. Trace amounts."

A lot of vehicles ended up with gunpowder in the trunk. People carried weapons there more times than made sense. Was it tied to all the break-ins, though? And if so, what did that mean? What were the would-be thieves after?

"I can be there in thirty minutes in street clothes or an hour in uniform."

"As long as I'm not staring at you in your tighty whities, I don't care what you wear. Just get down here. We're going to split the kids up and press them."

Dead air told Caleb the captain had hung up. With a turn of his key, the engine roared to life, and he left Lily's apartment building behind.

Twenty-One

"No. Doctor's orders." Lily stood, hands on her hips, and stared down a man who might well become the next president of the United States. "It's not happening."

"My request is perfectly reasonable."

"Allowing reporters into our ICU is as far away from reasonable as you can be. You might as well ask Agent Whitehall here to wear a pink tutu and perform pirouettes up and down the hallway."

The agent in question choked on the drink of water he'd just taken.

Jefferson David Taylor, still hooked up to an IV and with a blood pressure cuff in place, crossed his arms and lifted an eyebrow. "Word about the assassination attempt is out. If I don't make a public statement in some way, shape, or form, my opponents will have a field day with this. I'll be painted as on my deathbed, and my voters will jump ship and paddle to the next healthy candidate they can find."

"You give the American people too little credit."

"I understand your position, Lily. You're concerned about the privacy of the other ICU patients, right?"

She eyed him warily. "This is more than a concern. It's the law. We have a legal obligation to protect their privacy."

"Make sure the curtains over all their doors are closed."

"We have a wall-sized chart out at the desk with patient names on it. I can't close a curtain over that." Lily's foot tapped soundlessly on the composite vinyl flooring.

"Might I suggest..." Agent Whitehall sauntered over to the door and stole a look out into the bustling ICU. "We pick two reporters from opposing networks. One of my tech guys can stand in as cameraman. We'll use our own equipment, too. Let's say we allow a twenty-minute window. Secret Service clears the floor, and we set Taylor up in the waiting room so no one need enter the unit."

Lily started to object, but Whitehall raised his hand to stall her. "His nurse will be on hand. You can even throw a doctor into the mix if you want. Let the reporters ask a couple questions. Secret Service escorts the reporters out, my tech guy gives a flash drive with the interview to each of them plus one to the campaign folks so they can run with it, too."

Mr. Taylor stared at his hands for a moment in what Lily referred to as his thinking pose. When he looked up, his eyes held determination. "I like it. They may wonder if my health is the reason I'm not giving them free rein, but if you say it's a Secret Service directive, they'll be less inclined to claim I'm on my deathbed. That'll leave enough room for doubt that it might hold the vultures off from picking my political bones for a bit."

Lily sighed her defeat. "Let me check with the doctor. If he says yes, he'll take it to the hospital admin." She pivoted toward the door only to find Dr. Matsui standing right inside the threshold.

The doctor nodded to them. "It's a workable plan, and administration ordered our compliance when Taylor was first admitted. We're to support any wish to make a media appearance as long as it doesn't cast the hospital in a negative light." Dr. Matsui took charge and issued orders. "Tell your men to put it into play, Agent Whitehall. Lily, prep him. I want this over and done within the hour, or we call the whole thing off. The stress of drawing it out won't be good for the patient." The doctor stared hard at the man in the hospital bed. "My medical license is on the line if you're in front of the camera and this thing goes sideways. If you start to feel poorly, tell Lily immediately. Are we clear?"

Mr. Taylor nodded his understanding. "I'll drum my fingers on the wheelchair arm if something's wrong. That will be my signal."

Cloak and dagger was not Lily's forte. She rolled her eyes. "Fine. Let's get this over with."

Agent Whitehall began making calls to set everything into motion while Lily brought her patient a toothbrush and helped him into the attached bathroom. His ability to groom himself for the camera would be hampered by a hospital gown and the wheelchair he'd be forced to sit in, but they'd do what they could.

"In closing, I want the American people to know that I will not bow to intimidation, no matter how blatant it is. Those who are threatened by my fight to restore integrity to our political system and the White House have no power over me. I answer to a higher authority. I answer to the people of this great nation, the United States of America. My campaign is still in full force, and I hope to see each one of you at the polls. God bless you, and God bless America."

The interview had been interesting enough, but Lily was glad it was over. She waited for the Secret Service agent running the camera to give her the go-ahead. Then she stepped up to Mr. Taylor, released the brakes on his wheelchair, and wordlessly pushed him from the room. Dr. Matsui fell into step behind her, and Agent Whitehall came after him. The other agents would escort the two reporters back down to the lobby after they received their flash drives. Only time would tell what spin they'd put on things. It helped that Taylor's campaign would get a copy, too.

Lily was in the process of helping Taylor into his bed when a vibration reached her ears. Agent Whitehall took out his phone and glanced at it.

He bit out an expletive.

"What?" Mr. Taylor sat on the edge of his bed now.

The agent ignored him and entered a number into the keypad of his phone with enough force to make a lesser screen crack under the pressure. "It's Whitehall. Plan Delta is in effect. I repeat, we're a go for Plan Delta. When will you be at the rendezvous point? … I'll be there with the package."

As soon as he disconnected the call, Whitehall walked over and closed the room's door. Then he swung to face Mr. Taylor. Lily got caught in the crossfire of his intense gaze. "We might have a lead on the assassin, but if we're right, you're in bigger trouble than you know how to handle. You're under Secret Service protection, and you're going to let us do our job. At this point, any attempt you make to argue will be ignored. You will do as you're told. Period."

The color drained from Mr. Taylor's face, and he acquiesced with a dip of his chin. "What's Plan Delta?"

"That's classified."

"I have clearance."

"Not for this."

Agent Whitehall turned to Lily. "He's leaving this hospital in fifteen minutes. You won't change my mind. Neither will a doctor. Taylor won't be signing any forms, either, understand? No against-medical-advice documents. No paper trail showing he's left the building. Someone else is going to come in, climb into that bed, and pretend they've been shot. If you can't handle it, say the stress of the media got to you and take a couple days off. I need him in that wheelchair and ready to go."

Lily was tempted to quake at the imperial command, but she'd seen enough of Agent Whitehall not to take his tone personally. "He needs medical care. Insisting on taking him out of the hospital is bad enough, but removing him from trained staff that can monitor his recovery is something else altogether. You'll do the assassin's work for him."

The agent pulled a backpack out from a drawer next to the bed. "Put in here everything he's going to need for the next twenty-four hours. A doctor is waiting for us on the other end, and a combat medic will be traveling with us. Taylor will be in my care without medical personnel for sixty minutes tops, but load up anything you think we might need. Write down his medications."

"I… I can't access his meds in the time you've given me. The pharmacy won't fill the order that fast."

Agent Whitehall shoved a piece of paper at her. "List them. I'll relay the meds to the medic, and he'll get what we need."

One thing was clear. Mr. Taylor was leaving the hospital, and she couldn't do anything to stop him. Lily brought up the med schedule on the screen and hit the print button. She also printed out the most recent ten pages of his chart, showing all his vitals and detailed wound care. She rushed out of the room and collected the papers from the printer as Dr. Matsui crossed the threshold.

His eyes showed no surprise, and she began to wonder how many secrets the hospital harbored.

She returned to the room with the printouts, but the doctor and Agent Whitehall were gone. Mr. Taylor lay there, the picture of unflappable calm. Lily could see why he'd done so well in politics. Either nothing got to him or he was a good actor.

The backpack still sat on the foot of Mr. Taylor's bed, so Lily put the chart in it and set to work emptying medical supplies from the cart into its various pockets. She couldn't send the prescriptions, but she would make sure her patient had everything else he might conceivably need.

The second the agent returned, she handed him the med list. Then she nodded to Mr. Taylor, who eased off the bed and settled back into the wheelchair he'd only minutes ago vacated. He was strong and in good health other than the bullet wound. In fact, if it weren't for the high-profile nature of the case, he never would have been admitted to ICU. She'd been running into that a lot lately. So much for ICU being reserved for those patients who actually required intensive care. The hospital needed to revamp their security protocols before that would ever change.

"Take care of yourself and don't overdo it. If you want to live long enough to be able to run for president, you can't be your own worst enemy. Understand?"

"Yes, ma'am. And thank you, Lily, for all you've done. I know the media attention has complicated your life, and having to deal with this guy all day…" He waved at the Secret Service agent. "Well, that's not a walk in the park, either."

She gave him a smile. "Just doing my job. I wish you a speedy recovery and safe travel to wherever it is you're going."

Agent Whitehall stopped her from pushing the wheelchair through the door. "I'll take it from here. You're officially relieved of duty." He held out his hand to her. "Maybe we can catch up sometime under more ordinary circumstances."

Lily took his hand. "Be safe."

The two men veered left outside the hospital room. The normal exit was to the right. She resisted the urge to spy on them and instead began straightening up the room.

Arms loaded down with dirty linens, she rounded the foot of the bed and almost ran into a new Secret Service agent pushing a wheelchair into the room. "I'm returning Mr. Taylor to you."

Lily peered at the man in the chair. There was some resemblance, she supposed. Same hair, a similar skin color, but...

She shook her head. "Give me a second to make the bed."

Dr. Matsui entered the room with a purposeful step as she completed the task. He conferred with the agent before turning to Lily. "You can finish out your shift or leave. The choice is yours."

"I would have to take his blood pressure and temperature and do everything else and enter it all into Mr. Taylor's chart?"

The doctor eyed her shrewdly. "Of course. He is, after all, Mr. Taylor."

Lily met the doctor's eyes. "Will I be in trouble if I leave?"

His smile was brief but genuine. "Not at all."

"Won't everybody else on the unit know there's been a... uh... change?"

Dr. Matsui shook his head. "Your patient was taken for a stroll by one of his agents. Nothing else occurred. However, if you choose to leave, we'll be short-handed, and a replacement will be brought in from the float pool to care for Mr. Taylor here. A float pool nurse who hasn't worked on the unit anytime in the last week ought to do nicely."

For the first time since she'd come to live in this bustling metropolis, she wished her job didn't keep her so close to the nation's capital. At least she wouldn't be around to listen to the gossip. "All right, then. I believe I'll go home."

"Of course."

Twenty-Two

Caleb had prepared himself for a long day, but within minutes, all five teens crumbled. A couple of items had been in the trunk when they took the car, most notably a rifle in a case, a Taser, and a Sig Sauer P232. The idiot kids only knew the kind of handgun because the name was etched on the side of the barrel. They'd pawned the gear to buy the drugs they were high on when they sped by him out on Lee Highway.

One of the kids remembered the name of the pawn shop, and uniformed officers went to go question the owner and — hopefully — take the items into custody.

"So…" Captain Browning exhaled the word. "What does this mean?" These weren't the sort of cases their division of the state police typically dealt with. She had been handling patrol officers for years, and the eagerness to break a bigger case gleamed in her eyes.

"Did the lab find prints, too?" The last time Caleb queried Malik, the tech had hung up on him.

The captain grimaced. "Those kids made a mess of the car. Over a thousand prints collected, most of them smears and smudges left by our joyriders. They got a few clear ones that don't belong to any of them or to the car's owners. No hits in CCRE. One possible match to an old print in IAFIS. The lab is running it against international prints as we speak."

The Central Criminal Records Exchange — or CCRE — was Virginia's own database. No match meant whoever's prints were in the car either hadn't committed a crime before in Virginia — or hadn't been caught.

IAFIS, the FBI's fingerprint system, pulled from records nationwide. It covered a lot more territory, but "possible match" was at best iffy.

"What did you learn about the crime that IAFIS linked to that print?" The answer was within their grasp, and when she hesitated before answering, he was even more certain about it.

Two other troopers had been sitting in on their little powwow, but the captain told them to leave. Once she shut the door behind them, she wheeled to face Caleb, energy sizzling in the air around her. "A decade-old assassination in California."

His stomach dropped like a roller coaster after the final big climb. "Political?"

She shook her head. "A Silicon Valley mogul."

"Murder for hire?" Caleb withdrew his phone, the urge to call Lily overwhelming.

The captain glared at him. "Not a word leaves this room, are we clear? The computer gave our print a 20% probability of matching the one from the California case. That's not enough to be actionable. It's not even enough to be reliable. We wait for the international check to come back."

"How long till those results come in?" Caleb ground his teeth.

Captain Browning tapped her fingers on the desk. "The call should have come in an hour ago."

The shrill sound of her desk phone filled the air. She grimaced and yanked the receiver to her ear. "I told you not to disturb me unless... Very well... Put him through."

Caleb needed the name of the guy killed in California in order to research the case. He wondered if he should alert Nick. His old friend might be able to pull some strings and get them the complete file. The FBI would likely be unwilling to turn it over to them.

The captain slammed her phone down and stared at him.

"What?"

She opened her mouth, then closed it again. The vein on the right side of her neck began to visibly pulse. Her clenched jaw only confirmed his suspicion. The captain's temper was barely under control, and whatever she'd been told on the phone was the culprit.

"Were you ever going to tell me you're working for the attorney general's office?"

Ouch. Good thing he'd already submitted his final report since his cover was blown.

"How'd you find out?"

"None of your business."

He conceded the point with a nod of his head. "Sebastian was babysitting me instead of the other way around, wasn't he?"

The slight flare of her nostrils gave him the answer.

She gritted her teeth and ground out the words. "Give me one good reason not to throw you out of here this instant."

Caleb didn't plan to let her try. His gut told him to stick with this case, and that was what he aimed to do. "Your name came up during the course of an investigation into somebody else. The attorney general's office wanted to find out if the link was anything more than tangential. They needed to know where all the bodies were buried before they brought a case against the other person. No stone was left unturned. I just happened to come on the scene at the right time, and I got the job of investigating you and your station."

Her lips thinned. "I didn't hear a reason anywhere in your monologue." She picked up the phone. "Send the sergeant in."

Caleb held up his hands. "My final report's been turned in. Throwing me out won't change anything in that report, but it will put you a man down with a critical investigation heating up. Besides, I got permission to stay on until after the transportation hearing."

The sergeant opened the door, but the captain waved him off. "Give us a minute, but don't go far." Her eyes didn't leave Caleb's face as she spoke. Once the door clicked closed again, she demanded, "Why would you ask to stay on?"

"It was the right thing to do."

"Sneaking around my station was never the right thing to do."

He needed her to be reasonable. Not that he would be if their roles were reversed. "If you were in my shoes, you'd have done the exact same thing. In any event…"

Caleb's phone rang then, and they both jumped. A quick glance told him the call was from Agent Whitehall. He didn't bother to ask permission before answering. "This is Graham."

"Listen. You're in the middle of something. I don't owe you this call, and it's not professional courtesy. This is because I don't want your lady friend yelling at me if she finds out I had knowledge of what's coming and didn't warn you."

His eyes on the captain, Caleb demanded, "Spill it."

"Your signature is on a request for a fingerprint check. That print matches an international assassin on Interpol's most wanted list. The FBI is on their way to you now. For all intents and purposes, this case will be out of your hands as soon as they arrive. Secret Service is going to be working jointly with them — as jointly as we can, anyway. Your station will be swarmed in less than ten minutes, and the feds will want every single note, conversation, and scrap of paper that exists in relation to the print you ran."

Caleb nodded, even though Whitehall couldn't see him. "Thanks for the heads-up." International assassin... It had to be about Taylor. "Lily?"

"I have eyes on her and an agent in her building until this is resolved."

That would have to do for now. If the clock could be believed, she would still be at the hospital, which meant she was safe. "Is there anything else?"

"The FBI might ask for a liaison to local law enforcement. Make sure you get yourself appointed. I put in a good word for you."

"Understood." Caleb clicked the disconnect button on his phone and tried to repair the damage he'd done to the captain's trust in him. "International assassin, possibly related to the Taylor shooting. FBI and Secret Service should be here in minutes. The moment they arrive, we're off the case."

The captain surprised him with a smile. "Those kids stole the car before the job was finished. The timeline doesn't match the assassination attempt, so maybe our guy was scouting."

"What if there was a first attempt nobody knows about? Can we find out where Taylor was when the kids grabbed that car?" The possibility didn't sit well.

The captain grimaced. "Either way, the shooter never got the chance to clean the car up. We may have stumbled across the only lead in Taylor's shooting. That gives us a bargaining chip. The feds won't hijack this case away from me without a fight."

Caleb stood, rested his hands on her desk, and leaned in just enough to make his point. "My final report to the attorney general will be available to you within ten days. I found nothing of note. You run a tight ship, and you keep it clean." It might smooth things over if he told her the transportation chief hadn't come out smelling quite so good, but that information was still privileged. She would learn about that along with everybody else. When charges were brought. Captain Browning might even be called in to testify against her brother-in-law.

Caleb pressed her. "Let me stay with this case, and let me do my part at the transportation hearing."

She'd been under investigation without knowledge of it. It smarted, and he knew it. He wouldn't be any happier if he were in her shoes. At some point she would accept it as necessary, but he needed her to speed up that process and get to grudgingly-okay-with-it sooner rather than later.

"I'm not making any promises, but we'll table this discussion for now."

It was better than he'd hoped for. He'd take it.

Twenty-Three

Lily collected her things and was on the way to the elevator when Maddie chased her down.

"I thought I'd run into you in the break room, but it seems you're leaving early."

She tried not to mumble. "Yeah."

"Guess what?"

Lily looked at Maddie. Her friend was glowing. Something was up. "What?"

"Holden asked me to marry him."

Envy bit at her, but that didn't make sense. She was happy for them. "Congratulations! I mean, you said yes, right?"

"Duh." Maddie laughed. "So what's up? Why the early exit?"

Lily shrugged. "It's been one of those days." As explanations went, hers was filo dough thin, but she hoped her friend fell for it. "I have to go, but I can't wait to hear all about how he proposed."

Maddie smiled as the elevator doors opened. "We'll get together sometime and I'll give you the scoop. Right now a pile of paperwork is waiting for me. Both my patients are scheduled to go off-floor for tests."

Lily gave a small wave as the doors closed between them. She didn't envy Maddie. Most people had no idea how much work went into taking an ICU patient out of the unit for any kind of test or procedure. If the paperwork alone wasn't enough, all the portable equipment had to be put into place, the transport staff notified, the requisite respiratory tech acquired — especially if the patient was on oxygen — and, depending on the patient's condition, a resident might even be required to accompany them down. Coordinating so many people and moving parts ate up time.

The elevator began its descent, and she mulled the whole scene over in her mind. Why the envy? Sure, every woman wants to be loved, and every girl dreams of her wedding, but she'd not ever been the jealous type before.

She craved Caleb's presence. Lily was sure of herself when she was around him. When they were apart, she started to doubt this thing growing between them. Common sense butted in. Was she being sensible, though, or was she using sensibility as an excuse to keep him at arm's length?

Truth be told, she didn't want him at arm's length. Lily wanted him a whole lot closer.

The force of that want scared her.

I don't like being confused, God. I prefer clarity. You know that. Why am I so muddled where Caleb's concerned?

Shortly after Lily arrived home, her phone rang. Caleb's name appeared on her screen, and she smiled as she tapped the answer icon. Seeing his name brightened her mood. "Hey, there."

"Lily? I didn't expect you."

"Then why did you call?"

His voice apologized. "I didn't mean anything by it. I figured I'd be leaving you a message. You took me by surprise when you answered."

"I had an early day. I just got home. Are you working tonight? We could meet for dinner if you're not."

Caleb hesitated long enough for her to notice. "Dinner sounds good. Why the early day?"

"Are you sure about dinner? Do you need to head into work?" Hopefully he didn't notice that she was evading his question.

"Is everything okay at the hospital?"

So much for that. "Um, yeah, it's fine. I just… um… wrapped things up early today. No biggie. So about dinner…"

"Dinner's fine. I've been appointed as a departmental liaison to the FBI on a case, so my hours are skewed. I should be out of here around six. You pick the place and text me the name. I'll meet you at half past. Sound good?"

Liaison. Impressive.

"All right, but if something comes up, let me know."

This time his words held a smile. "I'll be there. Don't you worry about it. And don't worry about me, either."

He'd told her not to worry, so of course she had. What was he doing with the FBI that prompted him to tell her she didn't need to worry? Obviously something worth worrying about, or he wouldn't have mentioned it.

Lily sat at a table with a view of the front door. The red neon trim on the outside of the diner reflected off the shiny metal siding and turned everything an interesting shade of pink. Like most Fifties diners, it had a basic menu and an overabundance of retro wall hangings. No amount of kitschy décor, though, could detract from the best wet fries east of the Mississippi. Lily was contemplating those very fries on the menu when Caleb strolled in.

He scooted into his side of the booth and sighed. "You're a sight for sore eyes."

She'd secretly hoped for at least a kiss on the cheek when he arrived. Why'd she ever tell him no more kissing? "You don't look too bad yourself. How did your liasing go?"

"Is that even a word?"

Lily gave him her sassiest grin. "It is now."

Caleb's grey eyes danced. "Someone should appoint you lawmaker. None of this nonsense with things dragging out for decades in Congress. If you say it, it's the law. End of discussion."

"Forget it. I'd rather suture a wound any day."

Caleb moved his silverware from one side of his place mat to the other. That was the closest she'd ever seen him come to fidgeting. Something was up, and she probably wasn't going to like it.

"I should tell you, I don't work for the state police." He winced. "Well, I do, but I don't."

Lily rubbed her forehead. What on earth…? "So when you pulled me over, you were dressed in that uniform because you were on your way to a bachelorette party?" She was only half kidding.

Laughter turned his eyes silver. "Not exactly. It's complicated, and I can't tell you everything, but I can give you a bird's eye view."

She nodded, her insides tightening into a knot. Subterfuge wasn't her style. That was why she'd left the hospital rather than stick around and nurse the fake Mr. Taylor.

"I was hired as an investigator for the state attorney general. One of their ongoing investigations involved the state police. I'm new to the area, a blank slate. Getting in and doing the work was easy."

Lily resisted the urge to sulk, but her words still held a bite. "Isn't this sort of thing supposed to be kept secret? Why are you telling me?"

"My investigation's over. I'll be sticking around long enough to liaise and to testify in an upcoming hearing. Then I'm returning full-time to the AG's office."

"As an investigator?"

His head bobbed.

"Did you really work for a sheriff's department in rural Texas?"

"Yep, and I loved every minute." Could a person be this genuine and still be real? He made it hard to get angry.

"What happened to wanting to spend the rest of your life in law enforcement?"

A half-nod this time. "The AG enforces the law, and I'm in its investigative branch. I still get to do what I want. The red tape might kill me, but other than that, it's not so different."

"How does a small town cop land a job with Virginia's attorney general?"

"Connections. An old friend. I checked with him for an idea about where I should apply, and he suggested a position with the AG's office."

"He must trust you."

"We studied criminal justice together in college. Our lives took different paths, but we've stayed in touch. He came to my dad's funeral. I'd have told you sooner, but I was under orders to keep it quiet."

A smile tugged at the corner of her mouth, and she gave in to it. "I've lived around here long enough not to be surprised by too much. I even know where Congress's secret bunker is."

He lifted an eyebrow. "Secret bunker?"

"Where they'll be evacuated to if terrorists attack the Capitol. A patient got chatty on pain meds one day." She folded the wrapper from her straw and kept her eyes on the table. "This part of the country is full of secrets and hidden agendas, but for some reason, I didn't expect it coming from you. This is it, right? No other big surprises?"

He shook his head. "That's my biggie. Otherwise, I'm an open book."

Good. She didn't mind the occasional surprise, but she wouldn't want to live her life wondering where he was going each time he strode out the door.

Whoa. Where had that thought come from?

And fast on its heels came another... *Investigators wear suits.* Hm. As long as he didn't get rid of the cowboy hat, she supposed she could live with it... but she would miss seeing him in uniform.

The waitress took their order, and Caleb stretched his arms out on the back of the booth, striking a relaxed pose. "Something else is on your mind."

Lily bit her bottom lip.

"Tell me. Or ask, I guess, depending on what it is."

She might as well say it since she hadn't been able to stop thinking about it all afternoon. "I've been sending you mixed signals."

"You've been a little hot and cold, but like I said, I'm patient."

"I don't like the way I've been all over the map with you. That's not who I am. I want you to know that. I'm normally pretty stable and solid. I…"

He waited.

"…I'm not making much sense." She let out a heartfelt sigh. "Am I reading you wrong? I'm turning this into a bigger deal than it needs to be, aren't I?"

"You sure you want to talk about this?" Caleb's voice was guarded. "You told me not to bring it up any more."

"Yeah." Lily bowed her head briefly. "I need to figure this out. It's not fair to you if… I just want to understand."

"All right, but you asked. No getting mad at me because I'm talking about the future."

She nodded.

"If it was up to me, we'd be married within the week.

Lily's breath caught in her throat. He'd uttered the words so casually, but the heat in his eyes told her he meant every word. "How can you be sure I'm the one God has for you?"

"I don't know how to explain it except to say God and I have been discussing my wife for a long time, and I know."

"When were you sure? Before or after you gave me a ticket?"

He smiled. "By the time you drove off, I was trying to figure out how to make sure I was in that exact same spot every single morning until I saw you again. Then, later that day, there you were in Ma's hospital room, and it was a done deal. I knew."

The waitress arrived with their food, and once she left, Caleb bowed his head. "Thank you, Lord, for this meal and the time with Lily. I ask for wisdom as I manage this situation at work, and I ask for the safety of everyone involved. You're a mighty God, and I thank You today for being a God who keeps His promises. Amen."

Lily whispered an *amen* but couldn't take her eyes off him. "Is this work thing dangerous?"

He offered a half-nod. "In law enforcement, everything has the potential to become risky."

"But this has more potential than most situations?"

Another half-nod.

"Can you tell me about it?"

"Afraid not."

She bit her bottom lip but didn't argue the point.

"You got to ask me something. Can I ask you a question, too?"

Lily reached for a fry. "Sounds fair."

Caleb ate a fry before continuing. "Why are you having a hard time accepting that you ought to be filing for a marriage license? I realize I'm going fast, but when we were out there watching that meteor shower — or trying to — it felt like you wanted the exact same thing. Your change in attitude came out of nowhere, or at least it seemed that way to me. There had to be a reason, though. Help me understand."

Lily sat back. Hm. Rather than try to change her mind, he sought to understand her. What a novel concept. "Let me first say, I think I'm normal for hesitating to climb on your bandwagon. Most people would have trouble jumping into marriage — or even a serious relationship — so fast. Personally, I like to check things out before I jump in. The impression I gave you the day of the picnic... I don't know what to say. You kissed me, and I turned into this reckless, rash person I didn't recognize. And I liked it, which — when my senses returned the next day — kind of made me panic."

His eyes never left her face, and the warmth in them made her want to open up, so she continued. "I'm the woman who puts her toe in the pool to test the temperature. I plot my trip out on a map before I ever climb behind the wheel. That's my personality. It's who I am. I've been that way as long as I can remember. You, on the other hand, are a leap-before-you-look kind of guy. I'll bet you dive head-first into the pool without ever checking the temperature or looking for underwater boulders."

"In my defense," Caleb waved a fork to make his point, "pools rarely have boulders."

Lily rolled her eyes. "You know what I mean."

The corners of his eyes crinkled. "So our talking right now, this is you looking, right? You're checking the temperature, feeling around for boulders, doing all that stuff."

"I guess you could say that."

"Good. Ask all the questions you want, then."

She grinned at him. "So, what do you call your beard?"

He reached up and ran his hand over it. "This thing?"

"Yeah. It's more than a five o'clock shadow, but it's not a full beard, either."

His Adam's apple bobbed as he chuckled. "Well, this here is my ten o'clock shadow. It's a smidge past nine o'clock — which is a real beard style, by the way — but not quite an eleven o'clock."

"And is eleven o'clock shadow a real style?"

"Nah."

"So why that length?"

"You don't like it?"

Lily broke eye contact. "I didn't say that."

He shrugged. "It's long enough that my face doesn't constantly itch but not so long that I have to worry about combing it every day."

"If it matters, I kind of like it."

His eyes danced as a devilish grin showed his teeth.

The evening ended too soon for Lily, but when Caleb walked her to her car, she didn't mind. He wrapped his arms around her and gathered her in close for a hug.

This is what home feels like.

Her mind stumbled over the thought spoken by her heart. *Home.*

She stood on tip-toe and gave him another kiss on his scruffy cheek. "Errands are going to take up my day, but I can cook dinner for you tomorrow night."

Caleb's slow sexy smile sent a tingling sensation straight down her spine. "Sounds good."

Lily, still smiling to herself, pulled out of the diner's parking lot.

 Twenty-Four

Watching Lily drive away was flat-out hard. She didn't need to go off to her own apartment where she would have time to think up more reasons why they shouldn't move so fast. His opinion on the matter didn't hold much weight at present, though, and so he let her go.

He should have told her they'd be married within the month. But no. He'd said a week and meant it. Never mind that she wasn't ready to hear it.

She would come around eventually. She had to. His dad had once told him that he'd known he'd met *the one* when a single look from her could twist him up until he was inside out. And that was Lily.

On the bright side, the fact that Lily left work early was a good indication that Jefferson David Taylor was no longer in her care. Whitehall would have moved Taylor the second he got word on the print. In a perfect world, Taylor being out of the picture meant any possible threat to Lily was removed. They didn't live in a perfect world, though. And Lily wanted space. How could he protect her if she didn't want him near? Or was he overreacting?

His heart said to follow her. His brain said to leave her be. He couldn't hear his gut over all the noise the other two were making. A punching bag would come in handy right about then. In the past, whenever he'd felt that way, he'd gone over to his friend's cattle ranch and helped with the work until he was too exhausted to think. Cattle ranches weren't too plentiful in the metropolitan part of northern Virginia, though, so that was out of the question.

He ran a hand through his hair before deciding what to do. He dialed the phone as he climbed into his truck.

"Hey, Ma, don't wait up for me. I'm gonna stop at the gym on the way home... Yep, everything's fine. I have some energy to burn off... Will do. See you in the morning."

Caleb grabbed his workout bag from behind the driver's seat before going into the gym. He changed into shorts and a tank then stored the bag in a locker. He slipped his phone into its armband holder and threaded the cord for the earbuds through the appropriate spot so he could listen to his music while he exercised.

Once he got out to the floor, he went straight for the leg press. From there he moved to curls, push-ups, lat pull-downs, and eventually the chest press.

After one set, a woman sidled up to him. "Hey."

He nodded to her. "Hi."

"What're you doing?"

Caleb pinched the bridge of his nose before answering. "Working out."

"Oh," was all she said before she wandered off again.

The whole gym scene was awkward and uncomfortable. He'd not given fitness much thought before coming north. His life in general had been full of physical activity, but whenever he'd felt the need, a small weight machine stuffed into the back corner of the sheriff's locker room had sufficed. Since moving in with his mom, though, he spent too much time sitting around — usually stuck in traffic. Hence the gym membership.

After two more women approached him, he decided he'd had enough of the weights. He moved over to the cardio side of the gym and climbed onto the treadmill. Setting it for a steep uphill run, he started a steady jogging rhythm.

Less than a mile into the programmed routine, his phone rang. He widened his stance and rested his feet on the outside frame of the treadmill before slipping the phone from his holder. Hopefully it wasn't work. A quick glance at the screen told him that was wishful thinking. "This is Caleb."

"Whitehall here. Any developments on your end?"

"I'm liaising, but that seems to be FBI talk for fetching coffee."

"Please tell me you didn't actually fetch it?"

He snickered. "I, uh, brought them all empty cups with a map to the coffee machine."

Agent Whitehall laughed. "Wish I'd been around for that."

Silence fell, and Caleb rubbed his forehead. He appreciated the heads-up about the feds coming in, but Whitehall still liked Lily a bit too much for his comfort. "Is there a reason you dialed my number?"

The Secret Service agent cleared his throat. "I'm trusting my instincts where you're concerned. Don't make me regret it."

That phrase was becoming a steady refrain in his life. "Why don't you trust me with something worthwhile, then."

He sensed the agent weighing his words. "I've delivered the package to a safe location. I came back to the area because we believe the threat is still here."

Why was Whitehall telling him instead of the FBI? "Because there's another target or because the shooter is going to dig until he can reacquire the original one?"

"My guess? The latter."

Caleb's heart dropped. Lily. She'd never once said the name, but he'd known since the day he'd found Whitehall leaning against the side of his truck. Taylor had been her patient.

"Let me make a call." He hung up on Whitehall and pushed the button to bring up Lily's number.

He shut off the treadmill and began the trek to the locker room to collect his bag. His thumb hovered over the *send* button as he sorted out what to say that wouldn't frighten her.

When the phone vibrated in his hand mid-dial, he assumed the incoming call was from Whitehall. "What else do I need to know?"

"Caleb?" Lily's hesitation reached across the line and grabbed him by the throat.

"Hey. Sorry about that. I thought you were someone else. How've you been since I last saw you?"

Gridlock at the locker room's entrance tried to slow him down, but he forced his way through the tangle of bodies and hoped the phone didn't pick up the commotion following in his wake.

"Nothing. I… I wanted to say I had a lovely time tonight. You're a good man."

Don't spook her. "I enjoyed it, too, and the feeling's mutual. Only, I don't think of you as a good man. Where are you? It doesn't sound like you're calling from your apartment."

"I just got off the elevator. I'm almost to my door."

Caleb was jogging across the parking lot when Lily's sudden intake of breath reached him. He stopped midway to his truck, surrounded by the expanse of asphalt. "Lily? Lily, talk to me."

The gurgling sound of choking stretched over the line to meet him before the *kthunk* of her phone dropping rang in his ears. He pressed the phone as close as he could, listening. A couple of grunts, then the line went dead.

He ran the rest of the way to his truck, got in, and tore out of the parking lot before he processed any conscious thought of what he was doing. He had to get to her. He was the only one aware that she was in trouble. Caleb thumbed a button on his steering wheel. "Call Whitehall." He prayed the agent would pick up.

"Graham?"

"Lily's been attacked. The perp was waiting in her apartment. I'm twenty minutes away." Forty if he didn't plan on breaking every traffic law in the books.

An expletive came across the line, the agent's voice the verbal equivalent of razor wire. "I tried to check in with everyone on guard detail after you hung up. I can reach the man I have on the night nurse but not the one with Lily."

A burning heat started at the base of Caleb's skull and moved forward, but he fought it. Fear wouldn't help him — or Lily. She couldn't afford for him to succumb to emotion. Her life depended on it. If they were fortunate, the assassin didn't realize she was acquainted with anyone involved in the investigation.

Please, God. Keep her safe.

If the assassin did know…

"Graham, are you listening?"

Caleb, gunning the engine and swerving around a car that stopped for a yellow light, forced himself to focus on Whitehall. "I am now. What's the plan?"

"I've alerted backup and I'm on my way, but you'll arrive first. I'd tell you to wait, but you'd ignore me, so all I can do is warn you to proceed with caution."

"Do what you have to, but if Lily's been hurt…" So much for keeping his emotions under control.

Whitehall's resignation might have been comical in different circumstances. "Don't get yourself killed. That's all I ask."

Caleb ended the call and concentrated on the road. His clammy hands clutched the steering wheel in a death grip. He wove his way around the other vehicles as if he'd been driving in this craziness his whole life.

It was a miracle more traffic didn't clog the roads and hamper his way as he tore through the city. Yellow lights were ignored, and red lights became mere suggestions. An icy wind blew through Caleb's soul.

Please God. Keep her safe. Clear the roads.

The last thing he needed was an officer or trooper looking to ticket moving violations.

At one point he heard a siren, and his heart — already racing — jumped into triple-time. When it ended up being an ambulance traveling a perpendicular path on a street he was about to cross, he didn't know whether to sigh with relief or pound the wheel because his conscience forced him to stop and let it pass.

Caleb could have sworn hours had gone by since talking to Lily, but the clock on the dashboard told him less than thirty minutes had elapsed when he pulled his truck up to the entrance and jumped out. His hands shook as he reached for his off-duty weapon.

He couldn't go in skittish. He had to get a grip.

Cold fury filled him, pushing out all the fear, calming his jittery nerves, and steadying his hand.

Caleb closed his eyes for the briefest of moments. *Lily and I both need You, God.*

He pushed away from his truck, its engine left running, and raced through the lobby doors, badge in hand and weapon drawn.

Twenty-Five

Lily opened her eyes and took in her surroundings, frantic fear beating a rapid rhythm within her chest and filling her head with the sound of rushing wings, making it difficult to concentrate.

She was tied to one of her dining room chairs and was facing the kitchen.

She shook her head, and the movement shot hot pulses of pain rattling around inside her skull.

"I'm not going to bother introducing myself." The voice came from her right. "There are only two things you need to understand about me. I will find out where Taylor is, and I will kill you to get the information if necessary." The voice came from behind her now. "Do we understand each other?"

That voice… Something wasn't right.

Lily answered the question, but it came out as a garbled *yth*. It took her a moment to realize why she sounded so strange. Her mouth was taped. She closed her eyes and tried to focus, but her fuzzy memory wouldn't let her.

She'd phoned Caleb and told him it had been a good night. Or had he called her? Then what?

Her eyes flew open as her assailant ripped the tape away. A thousand needles of pain tore across her face.

"Where's Taylor?"

Lily forced herself to focus on the lithe, raven-haired woman standing in front of her. "I-I don't know."

The backhand was immediate. Lily's head snapped to the side, and the bitter taste of blood filled her mouth.

Wait. A woman? She'd been greeted at her own door with a chokehold, and it had been a woman?

"Where's Taylor?"

"Secret Service took him, but they didn't tell me where." Her attacker already knew he wasn't at the hospital. She wouldn't be in Lily's apartment otherwise.

Lily stared at her assailant. The voice matched the face — cold as ice and anything but masculine. She'd read too many books to not know how this would turn out. If she were blindfolded, she might have a chance at surviving the encounter. As it was, though, the odds were stacked against her. Witnesses rarely survived.

This time she expected the backhand. Being prepared for it meant nothing, though, in light of her inability to defend herself.

"One last time. Then we'll get serious. I'm not going to waste my time here with you. Where is Taylor?"

Lily wracked her brain trying to think of a plausible lie, but her concentration was broken by pain and fear. All she could do was shake her head and close her eyes as tears seeped out.

When no blow came, she cracked her eyes open.

Lord, save me. Shelter me, protect me, rescue me!

It was her only coherent thought. She gaped at the sight of her attacker in the kitchen, using tongs to hold a novelty biscuit-sized cast iron baking pan in the flames from the gas stove.

Bile churned in Lily's stomach and terror stole her breath. She fought to calm herself, control her panic, and force air back into her lungs.

The assassin examined her with a calculated smile. "If you scream, I'll make sure the children across the hall die gruesome deaths and that their last thought is about how you're to blame for their murders."

A buzzing sound started at the back of Lily's skull.

"What are their names again? Oh, that's right. Susie, Michael, and baby Lucie. Call for help, and you guarantee their end." She said it as though she were discussing the weather report.

The buzzing grew more insistent. Lily did her best to ignore it. "I don't know where he is. Ask me anything else."

"All right. We can play this game. Have the authorities identified me?"

Lily shook her head. "I d-don't think so. They didn't know who... who was behind the shooting."

"Do they have any suspects? What names have you heard?"

She shook her head again. "I... I haven't heard any... any names."

"You sure you didn't overhear Secret Service mention anyone?"

"No..."

The assassin made a choking sound. "Secret Service should have stayed out of it." She shoved the small round baking dish — approximately three inches in diameter — directly down into the fire, no longer bothering to hold it aloft with the tongs. She approached Lily, grabbed a nearby roll of duct tape, and tore off a new piece. The assassin snugged the fresh tape tightly against Lily's mouth.

She leaned casually against the counter that separated them from the kitchen. "I was hired to do a job, and I always finish what I start. Don't bother asking who hired me, either." She leaned forward long enough to touch a finger to Lily's taped mouth. "After all, every girl should keep a few secrets.

"When a job came up in the U.S., I knew I should have declined. The money was too good to turn down, though. Dumb of me, really. Jobs in the

U.S. never go the way I envision them. Too late to do anything about that now, though."

She crossed her arms and continued leaning against the counter. "I was scouting a possible site to complete the job when somebody stole my car. I pride myself on not leaving a trail, so you can imagine my upset when that car ended up in the hands of the state police."

With a shake of her head, the assassin moved back into the kitchen. She used the tongs to remove the baking dish from the stove's flames, then walked deliberately toward Lily.

Tied to the chair, Lily could do nothing but listen and watch as the woman came closer and closer. The dish was supposed to bake biscuits so they came out with the imprint of a snowflake on the top. A gift from someone at church. She'd never even used it. Who baked just one biscuit?

Lily fought the hysteria bubbling its way to the surface.

"I believe you, I do. You understand, though, that I have to be certain?" The woman's voice grew sinister. "So this is your last chance. Nod if you're ready to tell me where they took Taylor. Or you'll be branded for life."

Or death. Lily shook her head frantically, choking on her own sobs.

Twenty-Six

Caleb approached Lily's apartment door. He stood as close as he dared, listening for any hint of what went on within the walls, but no distinguishable sound came through the door. Seeing no other course of action, he shot the lock and kicked the door in. His gunfire echoed in the hall, an almost deafening roar.

Backup was already on the way, but he hoped every neighbor within hearing distance was on the phone to 911. The woman he loved was in danger, which meant there would never be enough backup to suit him.

He charged over the threshold. A woman stood over Lily with… a branding iron? Whatever it was, she had it in one hand and her gun in the other. If he fired, the woman could drop whatever she was holding right onto Lily. So he rushed her. The woman flung the metal contraption at him. He dodged it, but with too much momentum built up to stop, he had no hope of avoiding her gunfire. Pain seared through his shoulder and arm as he hit her full-force, tackling the internationally wanted assassin like the linebacker he'd never been.

They went flying past where Lily was secured and crashed into the wall with enough force to spew plaster dust into the air. The jarring impact rattled every bone in his body and sent pain pulsing through his right side with each beat of his heart. He still gripped his gun, though, which meant this was far from over. Caleb backed away slowly and kept his weapon trained on the woman. Her hands were empty. The gun she'd used must have gone flying when he'd tackled her, but he had no way of knowing where it had landed.

When he saw Lily out of the corner of his eye, he implored her, "Nod if you're okay."

She nodded, and the relief almost brought him to his knees.

Caleb was reaching for one of the pairs of restraints he'd tucked into the pocket of his gym shorts when a door opened out in the hallway and someone screamed. After so much gunfire in close quarters, his ears were ringing, and the scream was muffled. His attention was jerked away from the assailant for an instant, not even long enough to turn around and look toward the scream. It was, however, long enough for Lily's captor to reach her ankle holster. He registered the movement and years of training came to the fore. Caleb kicked Lily's chair to the side and fired three shots in a tight cluster. The woman also pulled the trigger, but she only got one shot off before she collapsed like a rag doll on the apartment floor. His left arm felt like someone had stuck him with a fireplace poker, evidence that her shot hadn't gone as wild as he'd hoped — or hit the woman he loved.

He made a move toward Lily, but the roar of thunder penetrated his still-ringing ears and gave him pause.

Men in black tactical gear swarmed into the room. "ON YOUR KNEES! DROP THE GUN!"

Not thunder, then. Boots. The cavalry had arrived.

Apparently Whitehall didn't kid around about backup. No apartment security, and no street cops. The Secret Service agent had sent an entire SWAT team.

Caleb set his weapon down then kneeled, putting his hands on his head. His right hand barely made it. One of those bullets had to have gone straight through his deltoid. Nothing about it felt life-threatening, though. Just painful.

None too gently, someone shoved Caleb to his stomach with a boot between the shoulder blades and restrained his hands behind his back with nylon cuffs.

Youch! With his arms forcibly held in place, there was no relief for the pull on his muscles.

Medics filed into the room next. After confirming the woman on the floor was dead, they saw to Lily.

Beautiful Lily. Alive and safe.

He would wait as long as it took. If she needed distance, she could have it. Caleb had been rushing things with her. By her standard, anyway.

She was the one for him. He still knew it. Now that she wasn't in danger, though, she could take all the time she wanted. They would go on dates, share ice cream, enjoy the movies, and spend sunny afternoons at the park playing Frisbee. Whatever she wanted. She was worth it. If she needed to be wooed, he would woo her.

The minute they tore the tape from her mouth, Lily scolded everyone within hearing. "Caleb works for the police... He saved my life... She's an assassin!" The fact that they wielded big guns and outnumbered her ten to one didn't faze her in the least.

Nobody argued the implausibility outright, but a couple of the men from SWAT snickered. Nothing about Lily screamed out *assassin's victim*. Her story was improbable. Unbelievable, even. Yet it was true, every last word.

The medics wouldn't let Lily out of their grasp. "I'm fine... I'm a nurse, for pity's sake... I think I'd know if I was injured... Why aren't you people checking on Caleb? Leave me alone... He's the one bleeding!"

He lay where he'd landed, cream-colored carpet fibers tickling his nose.

She's worried about me.

Warmth started in his middle and spread until it filled all his limbs, pushing away the cold, shaking terror from earlier and the burning hot rage he'd experienced when he'd seen the assassin standing over the woman he loved. Pretty soon all that remained was the warm glow of knowing Lily cared. That and the pain in one shoulder and both arms, pain that was officially graduating from burning to white-hot.

From the corner of his eye, Caleb caught sight of a new pair of shoes entering the room. Dress shoes, not tactical boots. The shoes moved closer, and the man wearing them squatted down next to him. "Wipe that silly grin off your face. You're making the SWAT guys think you're a deranged psycho killer." Whitehall's voice was a welcome addition.

"She's worried about me."

The agent's laugh snapped through the room like the crackle of lightning. All the intense energy that had been humming through the place vanished, burned up in an instant as the adrenaline level in the room shifted from *rush* to *aftermath*. "Let her go, guys. Changing her mind is a hopeless cause, and she doesn't want to be fussed at. Might as well let him up, too. He's one of the good guys."

Twenty-Seven

The moment those medics let go, Lily jumped to her feet and sprinted across the room. She threw herself at Caleb. Someone had removed his cuffs, but he was only halfway up off the floor when her body met his.

A misplaced ottoman behind his knees kept him from being knocked back-first onto the carpet. Instead, he fell into the ottoman and landed ungracefully on his derriere, Lily in his lap. All things considered, it wasn't a bad landing.

She wrapped her arms around his neck and pressed her lips to his. She poured all the emotions churning, bubbling, and raging inside her into that kiss, and he absorbed each one without complaint. Her fear, anxiety, and anger melted away in the face of his solid strength and unyielding love.

Husbands, love your wives… as Christ loved the church…

No one has greater love than this, that someone would lay down his life…

The Bible verses filtered into her mind without any conscious thought on her part.

She broke off the kiss and leaned back.

Is that You, God?

It wasn't normal to hear from God in the middle of passionately kissing a man in front of a room full of witnesses. Was it?

What God has joined together...

Hm. Maybe it was.

Lily couldn't deny it any longer. She'd known almost as quickly as Caleb, but she'd battled against how right it had felt. Maybe because she was cautious. Or because she was stubborn and didn't like being told what to do. Either way, her fighting days were over. She was ready to accept their future.

She released her grip on his shirt and brought her hands up to cup his face. The scratch of his ten o'clock shadow tickled her palms. No harm in one more kiss... "Marry me. Now. Today. Tomorrow. As soon as we can get the license."

His grey eyes widened, and she saw her future in them. They would be stronger together than apart. Life would come and they would face it head-on, hand in hand.

Caleb lifted his hands from where they rested on her hips and tangled them into her hair, pulling her closer. "I'll let you be the one in charge of when we get married, but you're coming home with me tonight."

Her cheeks warmed until they burned. Her resistance melted under the heat as she tried to think of something to say.

"I'm not leaving you alone again."

She started to shake her head, but he stilled her.

"Ma makes a great chaperone. We'll be in separate rooms, and she won't let us get away with squat. We'll go apply for the license first thing tomorrow, and you can call your family to invite them, but in the meantime, I need you somewhere safe."

Lily glanced over at the plastic sheet by the wall. She ought to be bothered by proposing marriage to a man in a room where lay the dead body of someone he'd shot. She wasn't, though. Right then all that mattered was that she and Caleb were okay and together, with a future brighter than any she'd ever dreamed for herself.

Caleb's words rumbled against her cheek. "I'm being irrational, and you don't like being told what to do. I know. Humor me anyway. Besides, I kind of ruined your door."

She trusted him. Plain and simple. She trusted him to keep her safe, to honor her, and to love her. "When can we leave?"

He growled, and Lily knew she would spend the rest of her life trying to find ways to evoke that sound from him. It was pure masculinity and one hundred percent Caleb.

His lips claimed hers again, and she fell into the kiss, knowing she was cherished beyond measure both by the man in whose arms she rested and by the heavenly Father who'd seen fit to bring them together.

The sound of applause slowly penetrated the fog of her thoughts, and Lily pulled away to glance around the room. Agent Whitehall gave her a thumbs-up, while the medics and tactical officers applauded.

They'd already been on their feet, so it probably didn't count as a standing ovation. In the future, when she retold the story to their children and grandchildren, though, it would include a thunderous standing ovation.

She glanced back at Caleb. He grinned at her, not at all embarrassed by the attention.

In fact, he looked downright smug...

Caleb leaned forward then and brushed his lips against her ear. "You're amazing, and don't you ever forget it."

The End

Author's Note

Thank you for taking the time to read *An Informal Introduction*. I hope you enjoyed Caleb and Lily's story. I had a blast getting to know them and the unique dynamic of their love-almost-at-first-sight relationship. And I have to admit, I enjoyed meeting Jefferson David Taylor and Agent Whitehall, too. Expect to see them again in the future…

If you can, please take a minute to tell others about this book by leaving a review on Amazon and Goodreads. I wouldn't mind if you told all your friends about it, too. Or took out an ad in your local paper… although that might get costly. In all seriousness, though, reviews are golden, and I appreciate every single one of them.

In the meantime, I would like to give a shout out to everyone who dedicates their lives to serving their fellow man by working in law enforcement. Let me also point out a couple of items I changed for the sake of expediency within this story. In the Virginia State Police, if a trooper or department is suspected of malfeasance, the issue is investigated by an internal agency. The state attorney general would not be involved. Nor would they send someone undercover to infiltrate the state police. In addition, the badge number I gave Caleb is fictitious. Actual Virginia State Police badge numbers have fewer digits. Because I didn't want to accidentally use a real trooper's badge number, I decided to change that up a bit.

I also want to take a quick minute to acknowledge the hard work of healthcare professionals across the country in all fields and forms. The work they do is tremendous, and the stress they are under is immense.

As any writer will tell you, gratitude is a common state of being in this line of work. I am beyond thankful that God gives me stories to share and the words with which to tell them. He has allowed me to do something I love, and it's a blessing every single day. Writing isn't a solitary journey, though, and I want to thank the people who have helped pull this story together and make it shine.

Thank you to Mike Unger for patiently answering medical questions from dosages to equipment and everything in between.

Thank you also to K.C. Turner, Elaine Morison, and the Information Office of the VSP. Their insightful — and sometimes humorous — answers to my law enforcement questions enriched both me and this story.

Lastly, thank you to the ones who cheered me on while catching all my dangling modifiers and missing antecedents: Elizabeth Maddrey, Shari Shroeder, and J. Gunnar Grey. You're each invaluable.

About the Author

Heather loves coffee, God, her family, and laughter – not necessarily in that order! She writes approachable characters who, through the highs and lows of life, find a way to love God, embrace each day, and laugh out loud right along with her. And, yeah, her books almost always have someone who's a coffee addict. Some things just can't be helped.

She takes joy in creating characters that, much like her, are *flawed...but loved anyway.*

You can find Heather online at www.heathergraywriting.com.

Other Books by Heather Gray

Informal Romance
An Informal Christmas
An Informal Arrangement
An Informal Introduction
An Informal Date (coming Fall 2016)
An Informal Affair (coming Spring 2016

Ladies of Larkspur (Inspirational Western Romance)
Mail Order Man
Just Dessert
Redemption

Regency Refuge (Inspirational Regency Romance)
His Saving Grace
Jackal
Queen

Contemporary Stand-Alone Inspirational Romance
Ten Million Reasons
Nowhere for Christmas

An Informal Christmas
Informal Romance Book 1

Chapter One

Rylie ran for the elevator. A man in a faded denim jacket stood inside with the back curve of his left shoulder facing her. He didn't acknowledge her high-speed sprint in his direction. Nor did he stop the two brushed steel panels from sliding closed between them.

She thought of pushing the button and forcing the doors to reopen. Honestly, though, did she want to get stuck in a metal box with a man who didn't care about basic courtesy toward his fellow mankind? Not likely. Rylie huffed out an exasperated breath as she started up the stairs. Three flights up. It could be worse.

With a shove to the door, she exited the stairwell and stood on a narrow landing with skylights above and a view of the hospital's lobby below. Ten steps to the left, and she broke through to the hallway-of-no-return. Nobody came up to this floor unless they worked in one of the three departments exiled here. The first door belonged to the chaplaincy. The second led to the main office for the hospital social workers. The third door, decorated with construction paper butterflies and cotton ball caterpillars, was home sweet home — Child Life.

"I can't believe how rude people have become!" Rylie vented about the man in the elevator as she stepped past the colorful decorations and into her domain. Suzie, the part-time department head who kept their ship running tighter than junior size spandex on a burly linebacker, wasn't at her desk. Their offices were anything but spacious, though, so she was likely still within hearing distance. After all, what was a good venting without someone to listen?

"I was running for the elevator, but the guy inside didn't even wait for me. He let the doors slide closed. Because obviously it wasn't big enough for two of us." She left out the part about his back being to her. Absolving him of guilt wasn't high on her priority list at the moment.

Suzie emerged from The Vault, a nether region of their office used for storage. She dusted her hands off and frowned at Rylie. "We have company." She waved at the man following behind her. "This is Mr. York. He brought several boxes of stuffed animals for our kids."

No way. Not... Lots of guys wore denim jackets, right? It couldn't be the same...

"Sorry about the elevator. I got wedged into position by my dolly. I thought I heard someone calling, but by the time I turned myself around, the doors were closed and I was on my way up here." His voice reminded her of a lemon tart, decadent smoothness with a sharp aftertaste. For some reason, she found herself tempted to savor the sound rather than pucker. Too bad her mind was already made up about him. He might have proven interesting.

Guilt gnawed at her middle. *Sorry, God. I'll be nicer once I catch up on my sleep.* She sighed. *Okay, now I'm making excuses.*

"Yeah, well, no worries." Rylie waved a hand dismissively and slipped past him to reach her desk.

Had there been a dolly in the elevator with him? She didn't remember seeing one, but her single-minded irritation at the world might have prevented her from noticing it. She couldn't worry about that now, though. One of her kids was scheduled to start chemo later in the day. Two were going down for CT scans. Yet another had bone cancer that had led to discussion of amputation. The potential amputee didn't seem to mind — he was still at the age where scars were to be boasted about and *prosthesis* meant something super-cool and possibly cybernetic. His parents, on the other hand, were pushing the outer edge of hysteria.

And then there was Makayla.

In and out of the hospital most of her life, she was sixteen and full of spirit. Confinement to the pediatric oncology unit didn't suit her in the least. Makayla never meant to make trouble, but she always somehow managed to end up smack dab in the middle of it. This time she'd started a petition for Fourth of July manicures. Now every girl in the unit wanted one. In red, white, and blue. The fourth was in three days. How was Rylie supposed to find time to search for patriotic nail polish on such short notice?

She ran her fingers through her stick-straight black hair and sighed. It would have to come out of her own pocket, too. Suzie had reminded her just last week. The Child Life budget was maxed out. They were dependent on donations at this point, and nobody had anticipated the whims of a sixteen-year-old girl well enough to donate red, white, and blue polish.

"Uh, Rylie, did you hear me?"

She looked up from her desk. Suzie stood there, her wide green eyes expectant.

"Sorry, Suz. My girls all want their nails decorated with the stars and stripes, and I need to figure out how to make it happen. What did you say?"

Suzie shook her head. "Polish isn't in the budget."

"I'll work something out."

The hulking form of Mr. York remained over Suzie's right shoulder. Not that he hulked exactly. His was the wiry build of an Olympic swimmer, and if forced to guess, Rylie would put him at a hair shy of six feet tall.

Suzie waved a hand in their guest's general direction. "Mr. York here is planning on making monthly deliveries to us. He'd like to be able to coordinate with someone so he's better informed about the needs of our patients. I hoped you could be his liaison. You know, keep him up to date, that sort of thing."

"Liaison? Isn't that your job?" Rylie regretted the words as soon as they passed her lips.

The middle-aged woman shook her head as a shadow dimmed her eyes. "I'm part-time since the cut backs, remember? My job is to keep this department running, but there isn't enough time in the schedule for me to handle everything that needs attention. If I don't start delegating, I'm going to lose my mind."

Suzie wasn't to blame. The hospital, not her, had decided Child Life needed only a part-time administrator. To run the entire department.

Rylie sighed.

Working at a children's hospital affiliated with a much larger adult hospital had tremendous benefits. Their patients had access to treatments and equipment that a smaller facility on its own wouldn't be able to provide. It had its share of drawbacks, too, though. One such drawback was money.

Decisions were made based on profit, and the adult hospital — with nearly four times as many beds — dominated the spreadsheet. As a result, the children's hospital found itself in an indefensible position whenever budget cuts were discussed. If the adult patients didn't demand a service, that service was deemed unnecessary.

Times were hard, and it was apparent nowhere more so than in this forgotten corner of the hospital where everybody worked themselves into exhaustion so the patients wouldn't feel the pinch of reduced budgets and staff.

"Very well. Give me a second, Mr. York." Rylie booted up her computer and sent a message out on the intranet that Child Life shared with Social Work and the Chaplaincy. *Need red, white, and blue nail polish for the girls in Oncology. Anybody have some?*

She counted to thirty, hoping for a return message. None came, so she shifted her attention to the man who now leaned against the wall opposite her cubicle, arms crossed. As she did so, she prepared to send her computer into hibernation. The mouse hovered over the *power down* icon as a beep reached her ears. Her fingers flew across the keyboard as she typed in the command to bring the intranet chat box to the front on her desktop.

Dollar store by my house had huge display earlier in week. I'll check on my way home this afternoon. How many bottles?

Bless her. Blossom, the retired CEO of a successful technology firm, had realized too late that she couldn't stand retirement. She now volunteered as a chaplain to fill her time. Per her choice, she worked with adults in her official duties, but off-the-unpaid-volunteer-clock she did whatever she could to help the children's hospital.

Two of each ought to do it. THANK YOU.

She hoped those girls realized they wouldn't be getting flags and fireworks on their nails. Her skills were limited. It would be a good day if she remembered to paint one nail red, the one after that white, and the next one blue. If they were smart, the girls would give each other manicures and leave her, at best artistically challenged, out of the fun altogether.

"Ah-hem." The man still leaning against the wall cleared his throat.

A quick glance at the clock told Rylie she needed to be on her way. The first of the CT scans was scheduled to start in fifteen minutes. Scotty, an eight-year-old patient, had asked her to accompany him because his parents were at work, and he didn't want to be alone.

"Walk with me, Mr. York." She brushed past him hoping her voice hadn't sounded as cold to his ears as it had to hers. It wasn't his fault she'd been running nonstop since coming through the hospital doors hours prior — or that the day's race was far from over.

A second later, the yell came from behind her. "Watch out!"

Rylie spun around in time to see a previously stacked column of boxes tumbling in her direction. Of course. The boxes with the marbles in them. Who had piled those blasted boxes so high? No one in touch with their sanity would be foolish enough to... Oh yeah. She'd done it. Because they'd needed the room.

A speedy jump saved her from most of the trauma, but the edge of one box landed on her left foot. Her yell filled their small office. Meanwhile, one of the other boxes broke open. Marbles began rolling across the floor. Rylie, her lost balance tossing her in that direction anyway, managed to throw herself in front of the door as she fell. At least the glass-orbs-of-doom wouldn't wander out into the hallway and cause further catastrophe.

Whose brilliant idea was it to donate a hundred pounds of marbles to the Child Life department? Now she remembered. The international marble champion Rylie had convinced to visit the hospital and host a demonstration for the children one afternoon had been so moved by the experience that he'd donated thousands of choking hazards to them. The boxes had been stacked in the corner so long she'd almost forgotten about them. Until now.

"It's awfully narrow in here. I brushed against a box. Sorry." Mr. York held his hand out to help her up, but Rylie wasn't sure she wanted to move. Some falls – and crushed toes – deserved to be babied for a bit. The image of poor Scotty, afraid of the CT machine, popped into her head, though, and she couldn't ignore the outstretched hand.

The benevolent stranger and knocker-over-of-boxes started to speak again, but Rylie cut him off as she got to her feet. "I'm needed elsewhere. Walk with me, or it'll have to wait."

"Don't worry about the mess here, folks. I have nothing better to do with my time." Suzie's indignant muttering followed them all the way to the elevator.

"You should get your foot examined."

Being angry at him would be easier if his voice didn't make her think of sweet treats on hot summer days.

"A little boy is going for an NBD test, but he's terrified. My job is to make it bearable for him, even if that means limping all the way there and back."

"NBD?"

"No Big Deal. The kids classify any procedure not involving needles, saws, or drills as NBD." The children actually said needles or a scalpel. She'd thrown *saws* and *drills* into the equation to get under his skin. Looks like it worked. So why didn't she feel good about it?

"Oh."

Rylie took a deep breath as the elevator eased down another floor. The time had come to start acting her age. Or even half her age. She wasn't exactly getting off to a good start with this man.

She held out her hand. "I'm Rylie Durham, the Child Life Specialist assigned to the oncology unit."

His hand enveloped hers in a warm grasp. "Zach York. I'm... the guy who knocks over boxes, gets himself jammed into elevators, and..." He rolled his eyes. "And apparently forgets his dolly up in the Child Life office so he has to go back for it later."

It was a trial, but she afforded him a smile. "What brings you to us?"

His shrug was a study in nonchalance. "Another time, maybe." He pulled something from his wallet and held it out to her. "Here's my card. Drop me an email within the next day or two so I know how to get in touch with you. When I'm ready to order some items for next month, I'll contact you and find out what y'all need."

She took the card but doubted any communication between them would be as simple as he made it sound. This man had complication written all over him.

"Ignore my email at your own risk, Ms. Durham." His molasses eyes glinted with a hint of mischievousness. "Or you might find yourself with more marbles instead of whatever children in the hospital actually need."

The elevator *dinged*, and the doors opened smoothly near the entrance to Oncology. Rylie stepped out but couldn't stop herself from glancing back at him. "Are you coming?"

"Not today. I need to fetch my dolly." He pushed the button that would return him to the forgotten corner of the hospital, and the doors slid closed.

Hm. He wanted to help the kids, but he wasn't eager to see them. He was either uptight, emotionally detached, or she was reading too much into his actions.

Tempted as she was, she couldn't take time to psychoanalyze the handsome Zach York. A wheelchair rolled her way, accompanied by a nurse. "Scotty! Sorry I'm late. You won't believe this, but a tower of marbles fell on me."

The little boy giggled and pointed to the foot she was favoring. "Is that where it landed?"

"Of course it is. You know I'm the clumsiest person in the whole world, right?"

www.ingramcontent.com/pod-product-compliance
Lightning Source LLC
Chambersburg PA
CBHW032139190626
46814CB00005BA/1756